DOVER · THRIFT · EDITIONS

The Immoralist

ANDRÉ GIDE

TRANSLATED BY STANLEY APPELBAUM

DOVER PUBLICATIONS, INC.
Mineola, New York

DOVER THRIFT EDITIONS

GENERAL EDITOR: STANLEY APPELBAUM

Copyright

Bibliographical Note

This Dover edition, first published in 1996, is a new translation of the work originally published in French by Mercure de France, Paris, in 1902. The translator has also supplied a Note, a map and footnotes.

Library of Congress Cataloging-in-Publication Data

Gide, André, 1869–1951.
    [Immoraliste. English]
    The immoralist / André Gide ; translated by Stanley Appelbaum.
       p.   cm. — (Dover thrift editions)
    ISBN 0-486-29237-1 (pbk.)
    I. Appelbaum, Stanley. II. Title. III. Series.
PQ2613.I2I4813 1996
843'.912—dc20

                                         96-11669
                                           CIP

Manufactured in the United States of America
Dover Publications, Inc., 31 East 2nd Street, Mineola, N.Y. 11501

NOTE

THE COPIOUS AND VARIED literary production of André Gide (1869–1951; Nobel Prize for Literature, 1947) was basically a long, penetrating investigation of his own character and potentialities — so much so that his diaries are frequently referred to as his finest work of all. At each point of his career he championed his outlook of the moment, but these outlooks evolved steadily, leading to apparent contradictions; for instance, almost nothing in his earlier work announces his social consciousness of the later 1920s or his flirtation with Communism in the 1930s.

Gide's earliest creations were imaginative essays or philosophical tales about the role of the artist, written in a poetic prose. At the time he frequented the salons of the Symbolist poets, but felt confined by the moralistic, puritan upbringing he had received. His attempts to set his spirit free crystallized in the major book-length prose poem *Les nourritures terrestres* (The Fruits of the Earth; 1897), in which he preached a sophisticated hedonism. The next important step was his first novel,* *L'immoraliste* (The Immoralist; written in 1901, published in 1902), in which the main character and narrator, Michel, liberates himself from social constraints with a vengeance.

Although in real life Gide obviously did not follow Michel's willful path of destruction and self-destruction, he shared many of his character's egoistic leanings, and the book is filled with autobiographical elements. Gide was similarly stamped by his rigid religious childhood; he also loved and valued the Greco-Roman classics; he had a bout with tuberculosis on his first trip to North Africa (which preceded his marriage, however); he sold off an inherited estate in Normandy; he felt uncomfortable in the Parisian social whirl; and so on. In one important

---

*Gide always referred to this book as a *récit*, or narrative, reserving the designation *roman* only for *Les faux-monnayeurs* (The Counterfeiters; 1925/6).

v

respect Gide had already gone far beyond Michel: his proclivities for native boys had already attained physical satisfaction, thanks to no less a mentor than Oscar Wilde, who provided some of the elements for the character of Menalcas in the novel (a Menalcas, a worldly tempter, had already appeared in *Les nourritures terrestres*).

Gide's combined biblical and classical heritage is very much in evidence in *The Immoralist*. On the biblical side, for instance, Michel's three listeners are likened to Job's friends, and a quotation from St. John plays a crucial role in the story. On the classical side, Michel gives many of his friends names from the Greek and Roman classics, while his discovery of his own body's beauty at the mountain pool near Ravello is a direct parallel to the myth of Narcissus, which Gide had already made use of in earlier writings.

Although only the original French text can fully reveal this, because it is largely a matter of grammatical and lexical subtleties, *L'immoraliste* is also important as marking a decided (but not yet total) shift in Gide's prose style from a somewhat decadent floweriness to his later classical and noble clarity and lack of clutter.

There are lineages in Gide's work. *The Immoralist* shares themes and concerns with two of Gide's later novels, *La porte étroite* (Strait Is the Gate; 1909; conceived as a pendant to the first novel) and *Symphonie pastorale* (Pastoral Symphony; 1919), in both of which a catastrophe is provoked by the moral intransigence or self-deceit of the main character. Some of Michel's more reckless actions also prefigure Lafcadio's famous, and much more shocking, "gratuitous act" in the novel *Les caves du Vatican* (literally, "The Cellars of the Vatican," but known as "Lafcadio's Adventures"; 1914).

The present translation, absolutely complete, is also as literal as proper English will allow, word-for-word with the natural exception of formulaic idioms. The translation by Richard Howard (Knopf, 1970) achieves some of its smoothness by omitting a large number of words — at one point, even an entire crucial sentence — and consistently skips over such technical matters as the different kinds of leases on Michel's farmland; there are also a few minor errors obviously due merely to hastiness. On the other hand, the translation reprinted anonymously in *The André Gide Reader* (Knopf, 1971) adds a great deal of unnecessary verbiage by translating many phrases twice in a row in different terms, as if the reader needed all the help he could get! Neither of these translations bothers to gloss the North African terms in the text, even leaving them in their French transliterations; similarly, they both leave all but the most common geographical names in Gide's spelling.

The present translation prints the foreign terms in the proper English transliteration and glosses them in footnotes (all footnotes in the text are by the translator; some of them briefly explain cultural references that may no longer be familiar to the general American reader), and uses the forms of geographical names as they are printed in major atlases or (in some cases) in specialized maps and guidebooks. In addition, a newly prepared map of Michel's travels follows this Note.

MAP OF PLACES MENTIONED IN THE NOVEL

(except Granada, Seville, Madrid and Budapest)

in the sequence of their first mention

1: Algiers

2: Constantine

3: Angers

4: Paris

5: Marseilles

6: Tunis (& Carthage)

7: Timgad

8: Sousse

9: El Jemm

10: Sfax

11: Biskra

12: Malta

13: Syracuse

14: Taormina (& Castel Mola)

15: Agrigento

16: Naples

17: Paestum

18: Salerno

19: Ravello

20: Amalfi

21: Sorrento

22: Positano

23: Ravenna

24: Rome

25: Florence

26: Venice

27: Verona

28: Lisieux

29: Pont-l'Évêque

30: Alençon

31: Neuchâtel

32: Lausanne

33: Chur
    (Tiefencastel, Piz Julier
    & Samedan are
    between 33 & 34)

34: St. Moritz (in the Engadine)

35: Bellagio

36: Como

37: Milan

38: Palermo

39: Catania

40: Qairouan

41: El Kantara

42: Touggourt

43: Chegga

44: Kef Ed Dar

45: El Meghaïer (M'Raïer)

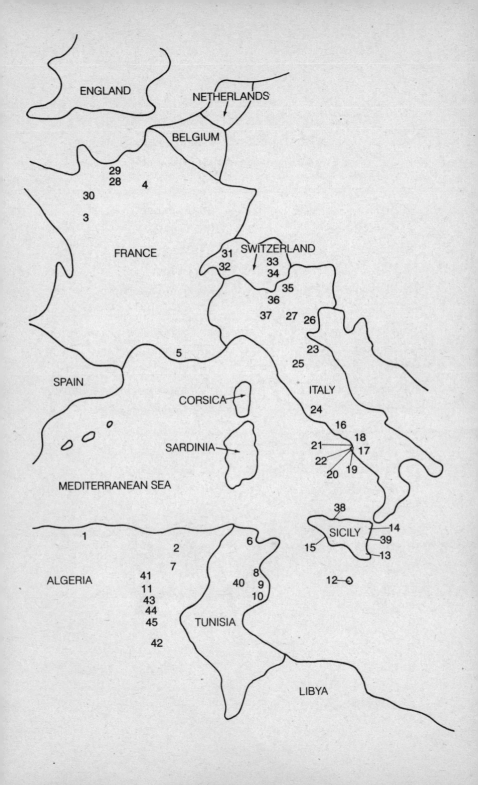

I will praise thee; for I am fearfully and wonderfully made.
(PSALM 139:14)

To Henri Ghéon, his loyal comrade, A. G.*

---

* Gheón was a writer associated with Gide on the magazine *Nouvelle Revue Française*.

PREFACE*

I PRESENT THIS BOOK for whatever it is worth. It is a fruit full of bitter ashes; it is like the bitter-gourds of the desert, which grow in sun-baked places and only offer the thirsty a more fearsome burning, but which on the golden sand are not without beauty.

Had I presented my hero as a model, I would clearly have failed badly; the rare individuals who were kind enough to take interest in Michel's adventure did so in order to denigrate him with all the strength of their own goodness. It was not in vain that I had adorned Marceline with so many virtues; readers could not forgive Michel for not putting her interests above his own.

Had I presented this book as an arraignment against Michel, I would scarcely have been more successful, for no one was grateful to me for the indignation he felt toward my hero; that indignation seemed to be felt in spite of my efforts; from Michel it spilled over onto me; there was almost an inclination to confuse me with him.

But it was not my intention in this book to produce either an arraignment or an apologia, and I refrained from making a judgment. The public today no longer forgives an author who does not declare himself for or against after narrating his story; even more, they would like him to take sides in the very midst of the action, to state a clear preference either for Alceste or Philinte,† for Hamlet or for Ophelia, for Faust or for Marguerite, for Adam or for Jehovah. I surely do not make the claim that neutrality (I almost said indecision) is a sure mark of a lofty mind; but I think that many lofty minds have been very unwilling to . . . draw a conclusion — and that to enunciate a problem clearly is not the same as imagining that it is settled in advance.

---

* The preface first appeared in the general trade edition, published a few months after the 300-copy special edition (both in 1902).
† Characters in *Le misanthrope* of Molière.

3

It is with reluctance that I use the word "problem" here. To speak truly, in art there are no problems — for which the work of art is not itself a sufficient solution.

If by "problem" we understand "drama," let me say that the one this book narrates, even though it is acted out in the very soul of my hero, is nonetheless far too widespread to remain confined to his unusual adventure. I do not claim to have invented this "problem"; it existed before my book; whether Michel is victorious or goes under, the "problem" continues to exist, and the author does not suggest that either the victory or the defeat is predetermined.

If some distinguished readers have refused to see anything more in this drama than the description of a peculiar case, nor anything more in its hero than a sick person; if they have failed to recognize that it might nevertheless contain some very urgent ideas of very wide interest — the fault lies not in those ideas or this drama, but in the author, and I mean in his incompetence — even though he has bestowed on this book all his passion, all his tears and all his care. But the intrinsic interest of a work of art and the interest that a transitory readership takes in it are two very different things. One may, I think, without too much conceit, prefer the risk of totally failing at the very outset to interest people in truly interesting things, to the greater risk of immediately gratifying a readership avid for nonsense, and thereby nullifying all influence on future generations.

All the same, I have made no attempt to prove anything, merely to paint an accurate picture and to give that picture the proper lighting.

To Mr. D. R., Premier of France

Sidi b. M.,* July 30, 189—.

Yes, just as you thought, my dear brother, Michel has spoken to us. Here is the story he told us. You had asked for it; I had promised it to you; but at the moment of sending it to you, I am still hesitant, and the more I reread it, the more horrible it seems to me. Oh, what are you going to think about our friend? And besides, what do I think about him myself? . . . Will we merely condemn him and deny the possibility that mental powers which bespeak cruelty can ever be molded for any good purpose? But there is more than one man today, I fear, who would venture to recognize himself in this story. Will we be able to invent a use for so much intelligence and strength — or refuse to allow them in our midst?

In what way can Michel serve the state? I confess I don't know. . . . He needs some occupation. Will the high position you have gained through your great merits, the power you possess, permit you to find one? Hurry. Michel is dedicated — he still is — but soon he will be so only to himself.

I am writing to you beneath a perfectly blue sky; in all the twelve days that Denis, Daniel and I have been here, not a cloud, no lessening of the sun's power. Michel says the sky has been clear for two months.

I am neither sad nor merry; the air here fills you with a very vague excitement and puts you into a state that seems as far from jollity as it does from sorrow; maybe this is happiness.

We are staying alongside Michel; we don't want to abandon him; you'll understand why if you go on to read these pages; therefore we'll be awaiting your answer here, in his home; don't delay.

You know that a friendship dating from schooldays, strong even at the outset but increasing yearly, has linked Michel to Denis, Daniel and me. A sort of pact was made among the four of us: at the least call for help from any one of us, the other three were to show up. And so when I received that

---

* Abbreviation for the name of a (probably fictitious) Algerian village.

5

mysterious alarm signal from Michel, I immediately informed Daniel and
Denis, and all three of us dropped everything and took off.

We hadn't seen Michel for three years. He had married and had gone
traveling with his wife; and the last time he passed through Paris, Denis
was in Greece, Daniel was in Russia and I, as you know, had to stay at
the bedside of our sick father. Nevertheless, we hadn't been left without
news of him; but the news given us by Silas and Will, who had seen him
again, had merely surprised us. A change was taking place in him that
we still couldn't understand. He was no longer the very learned puritan
he had formerly been, his gestures dictated by such conviction that they
became clumsy, his eyes so clear and bright that, looking into them, we
often curtailed our overly loose remarks. He was . . . but why describe to
you what his own story will tell you?

Therefore, I am sending you this story just as Denis, Daniel and I heard
it: Michel told it on his terrace while we were stretched out near him in the
darkness and in the starlight. At the end of the story we saw day breaking
on the plain. Michel's house overlooks it and also the village, from which
it is not far distant. With the heat, and with all the crops reaped, that plain
resembles the desert.

Michel's house, though bare and strange, is charming. In the winter
the cold was painful because the windows have no glass; or rather, there
are no windows at all, only huge holes in the walls. Now the weather is so
beautiful that we sleep outdoors on mats.

Let me add that our journey here was a good one. We arrived in the
evening, exhausted with the heat, intoxicated by the newness of things,
since we had stopped only very briefly at Algiers, then at Constantine.
From Constantine another train took us to Sidi b. M., where a small
open carriage was waiting. The road gives out far from the village, which
is perched on top of a rock like certain towns in Umbria. We ascended
on foot; two mules had been loaded with our luggage. When you arrive
along that road, Michel's house is the first one in the village. A garden enclosed by low walls, or rather a farmyard, surrounds it, in which
three warped pomegranate trees and a superb oleander grow. A Kabyle
child was there who ran away as soon as we came up, scaling the wall
unceremoniously.

Michel greeted us without displaying any joy; he was very straight-
forward, and seemed to fear any exhibition of warm feelings; but on the
threshold, at the outset, he embraced each of us solemnly.

Until nightfall we didn't exchange a dozen words. A dinner that was all
but frugal was ready in a parlor whose sumptuous decorations surprised
us, but which you will find explained in Michel's story. Then he served us

coffee, which he took the pains to make himself. Then we ascended to the terrace, from which the view extended to infinity, and all three, like the three friends of Job, waited, admiring the swift setting of the sun over the fiery plain.

When it was night, Michel said:

PART ONE

I

MY DEAR FRIENDS, I knew you were loyal. You have come running at my call, just as I would have done at yours. And yet it's three years since you saw me last. May your friendship, which is so unshaken by absence, also prove unshaken by the story I want to tell you. For, if I summoned you suddenly, and had you travel all this way to my distant residence, it was solely to see you and so that you could hear me out. I want no other aid than that: to talk to you. For I have reached a point in my life beyond which I can no longer go. And yet it's not out of weariness. But I no longer understand. I need . . . I need to speak, I tell you. To be able to free oneself is nothing; the hard part is being able to live with one's freedom. Allow me to talk about myself; I'm going to tell you about my life, simply, without modesty and without pride, more simply than if I were talking to myself. Listen:

The last time we met, as I recall, was in the outskirts of Angers, in the little country church where my marriage was being celebrated. Very few people attended, and it was the quality of my friends which turned that ordinary ceremony into a truly moving one. I felt as if the guests were emotionally stirred, and that stirred me. In the house of the woman who was becoming my wife, a brief meal, without laughter and without shouting, reunited you with us after we left the church; then the carriage we had ordered took us away, in accordance with the custom that makes our minds associate the idea of a wedding with the vision of a departure.

I was very slightly acquainted with my wife and, without being too hurt by it, I felt that she didn't know me, either. I had married her without love, largely to please my father, who, when dying, was worried about leaving me alone. I loved my father dearly; my mind absorbed by his imminent death, my only thought in those sad moments was to make his end more bearable; and so I mortgaged my life without knowing

9

what life could be. Our betrothal at the dying man's bedside was without laughter, but not without a solemn joy, because the peace of mind it gave my father was so great. If I didn't love my fiancée, I can say that at least I had never loved any other woman. In my eyes that was enough to guarantee our happiness; and, not yet knowing myself, I thought I was devoting myself entirely to her. She was an orphan, as well, and was living with her two brothers. Her name was Marceline; she was barely twenty; I was four years older than she.

I said I didn't love her at all — at least I didn't feel for her anything of what is called love, but I did love her if that can be taken to mean kindly feelings, a sort of pity and, lastly, a fairly great esteem. She was Catholic and I am Protestant . . . but I thought that that allegiance meant so little to me! The priest accepted me, I accepted the priest; it all went off without any major hitch.

My father was what is called an "atheist" — at least I imagine so, because, through a kind of unconquerable shyness, which I'm certain he shared, I was never able to chat with him about his beliefs. My mother's solemn Huguenot instruction had slowly faded from my heart, along with her beautiful image; you know I was young when I lost her. I did not yet suspect what great power that early childish morality has over us, nor what traits it leaves in our mind. That sort of austerity, a taste for which my mother had left to me while inculcating its principles, I transferred in its entirety to my studies. I was fifteen when I lost my mother; my father took charge of me, lavished his attention on me and made it his ardent goal to educate me. I already knew Latin and Greek well; with him I quickly learned Hebrew, Sanskrit and finally Persian and Arabic. When nearly twenty I was so well coached that he took the chance of making me a partner in his labors. It amused him to claim I was his equal, and he wanted to prove it to me. The *Essay on Phrygian Cults*, which was published under his name, was my work; he had scarcely looked through it to make revisions; nothing else ever garnered so much praise for him. He was delighted. As for me, I was embarrassed at the success of that hoax. But from that time on my career was launched. The most learned scholars treated me as their colleague. I smile now at all the honors bestowed on me. . . . And so I reached the age of twenty-five practically without ever having looked at anything but ruins or books, and totally ignorant of life; I applied unusual fervor to my work. I loved a few friends (you among them), but it was the idea of friendship I loved rather than the people themselves; my devotion to them was great, but it was from a need to feel myself noble; I cherished each fine feeling in myself. Anyway, I knew my friends as little as I knew myself. Not for a moment did it ever occur to me that I might have been able to lead a different life, or that a different life was even possible.

My father and I were satisfied with simple things; both of us spent so little that I turned twenty-five without knowing we were rich. Without thinking about it too often, I supposed we had just enough to live on; and, at my father's side, I had formed such thrifty habits that I was almost embarrassed when I realized we possessed much more. I was so withdrawn from such things that it wasn't even after my father's death, though I was his sole heir, that I began to evaluate my fortune a little more clearly, but only at the moment of my marriage contract, noticing at the same time that Marceline was bringing me next to nothing.

Another thing I didn't know, something perhaps even more important, was that my health was very delicate. How was I to have found that out, seeing that I had never put it to the test? I had colds now and then, and didn't take good care of them. The excessively tranquil life I led was weakening me and sheltering me at the same time. Marceline, on the other hand, seemed robust — and we were soon to learn that she was more so than I.

On the very evening of our wedding we slept in my Paris apartment, where two rooms had been prepared for us. We stayed in Paris only as long as was necessary to make indispensable purchases, then we traveled to Marseilles, from where we immediately took ship for Tunis.

The urgent preparations, the dizzying recent events that had occurred too fast, the unavoidable excitement of the wedding coming so soon after the more real emotion caused by my bereavement — all that had exhausted me. It was only when on the boat that I could tell how tired I was. Up to then, every bit of business, while increasing my fatigue, took my mind off it. The compulsory leisure of shipboard finally allowed me to reflect. It seemed to me that it was for the first time.

Thus, for the first time I was consenting to do without my work for a considerable period. Until then I had only allowed myself short vacations. A trip to Spain with my father, shortly after my mother's death, had lasted over a month, it's true; another one, to Germany, six weeks; and others — but those were study trips; while on them my father never forgot his very specialized research; and I, whenever I wasn't joining him in it, would be reading. And yet, scarcely had we left Marseilles when various memories of Granada and Seville came back to me, memories of a clearer sky, deeper shadow, festivals, laughter and song. "That's what we're going to rediscover," I thought. I walked up onto the ship's deck and watched Marseilles fade into the distance.

Then, suddenly, it occurred to me that I was neglecting Marceline a little.

She was seated forward; I came up to her and, actually for the first time, looked at her.

Marceline was very pretty. You know that; you saw her. I reproached myself for not having noticed it at first. I knew her too well to see her with fresh eyes; our families had always been connected; I had watched her grow up; I was used to her gracefulness. . . . For the first time I was surprised, so great did that gracefulness appear to me.

Over a simple black straw hat she had attached a large floating veil; she was blonde but didn't look frail. Her matching skirt and bodice were of a plaid shawl fabric that we had picked out together. I had refused to see my mourning cast a shadow over her.

She felt that I was looking at her and turned around to face me. . . . Up to then my attentions toward her had been consciously willed; to the best of my ability I substituted for love a kind of cold politeness that, as I clearly saw, troubled her a little; did Marceline feel at that moment that I was looking at her in a different way for the first time? In her turn she stared at me; then, very tenderly, smiled at me. Without a word I sat down next to her. Up to then I had lived for myself or at least in my own fashion; I had married without imagining that my wife would be anything more than a comrade, without thinking very clearly that, after our union, my life could be changed. I had just come to understand, finally, that the monologue was now over.

The two of us were alone on the deck. She held out her forehead to me; I clasped her to myself gently; she raised her eyes; I kissed her on the eyelids, and suddenly, through the agency of my kiss, I felt a kind of new pity; it seized me so violently that I couldn't restrain my tears.

"What's wrong with you?" said Marceline.

We started to talk. Her charming remarks delighted me. I had come to some conclusions, as far as I could, about the foolishness of women. Alongside her, that evening, it was I who felt awkward and stupid.

So then, the woman I was taking into my life possessed her own, real life! The magnitude of that idea awakened me several times that night; several times I sat up on my bunk to watch Marceline, my wife, sleeping on the other bunk below.

The next day the sky was splendid, the sea nearly calm. A few conversations devoid of urgency made us even less embarrassed with each other. The marriage was really beginning. In the morning of the last day of October we disembarked at Tunis.

My intention was to stay there only a very few days. I will confess my foolishness to you: nothing in this brand-new country attracted me except Carthage and some Roman ruins: Timgad, which Octave had spoken to me about, the mosaics in Sousse and especially the amphitheater at El Jemm, to which I decided to hasten without delay. It was necessary to reach Sousse first, then from Sousse to take the mail coach; in my mind nothing in between was worthy of my attention.

And yet Tunis was very surprising to me. As I came into contact with new sensations, parts of me were stirred, dormant faculties that had not yet been put to use, and so had kept all their mysterious youthfulness. I was more surprised, amazed, than amused, and what I especially liked was Marceline's joy.

However, my fatigue was increasing daily; but I would have found it shameful to give in to it. I was coughing and I felt a strange discomfort high up in my chest. "We're heading south," I thought; "the warmth will set me right."

The couch to Sfax leaves Sousse at eight in the evening; it crosses El Jemm at one in the morning. We had reserved the compartment seats. I expected to find an uncomfortable rattletrap; on the contrary, we were quite at our ease there. But the cold! . . . Through what childish trust in the gentleness of a southern atmosphere had we dressed so lightly and taken along only a shawl? As soon as we left Sousse and the shelter of its hills, the wind started to blow. It made great leaps over the plain, it howled, whistled, came in through every crack of the doors; nothing could protect us from it. We arrived chilled through; I, in addition, was exhausted by the jolting of the vehicle and by a horrible cough that shook me even more. What a night! When we got to El Jemm, there was no inn; instead there was a frightful burj.* What were we to do? The coach was leaving again. The village was asleep; in the night, which appeared immense, the gloomy bulk of the ruins could vaguely be made out; dogs were howling. We went back into a grubby room in which two miserable beds had been placed. Marceline was shivering with the cold, but there at least the wind no longer reached us.

The next day was a dreary one. We were surprised, when we walked

---

* Blockhouse.

out, to see a uniformly gray sky. The wind was still blowing, but less violently than the day before. The coach was not due to return before evening. . . . I tell you, it was a mournful day. The amphitheater, which it took me only a few minutes to examine, disappointed me; I even found it ugly, under that dismal sky. Perhaps my fatigue was abetting, increasing my displeasure. Toward the middle of the day, for lack of anything to do, I came back there, seeking in vain for some inscriptions on the stones. Marceline, sheltered from the wind, was reading an English book she had fortunately brought along. I came and sat down beside her.

"What a dull day! You aren't too bored?" I said to her.

"No. As you see, I'm reading."

"What did we come here for? You aren't cold, at least?"

"Not too. And you? Yes! You're extremely pale."

"No."

At night, the wind became strong again. . . . Finally the coach arrived. We set out once more.

From the very first jolts I felt worn out. Marceline, very tired, quickly fell asleep on my shoulder. "But my cough will wake her up," I thought and, working myself loose gently, gently, I left her leaning against the coach wall. However, I wasn't coughing any more; no, I was spitting; that was new; the expectoration cost me no effort; it came in short spurts, at regular intervals; it was such an odd sensation that at first it almost amused me, but very soon I was disgusted by the unknown taste it left in my mouth. Before long my handkerchief was no longer usable. My fingers were already full of the stuff. Should I awaken Marceline? . . . Fortunately I remembered a large scarf she was wearing around her waist. I took hold of it gently. The gobs of spit, which I could no longer keep back, were coming more copiously. I was extraordinarily relieved by that. "That's the end of my cold," I thought. Suddenly I felt very weak; my head started to spin and I thought I was going to faint. Should I wake her up? . . . Oh, imagine! (I think I have retained from my puritan childhood a hatred for any kind of concession to weakness; I immediately call it cowardice.) I took hold of myself, I tensed myself, and finally overcame my dizziness. . . . I thought I was back on the sea, and the noise of the wheels became the noise of the waves . . . but I had stopped spitting.

Then I slipped into a kind of slumber.

When I came out of it, the sky was already full of dawn; Marceline was still sleeping. We were getting near. The scarf I was holding was of a dark shade, so that I noticed nothing at first; but when I pulled out my handkerchief again, I was amazed to see that it was full of blood.

My first thought was not to let Marceline see that blood. But how? I was stained with it all over; now I saw some everywhere, especially on my fingers. . . . I had probably had a nosebleed. . . . "That's it; if she asks about it, I'll tell her I had a nosebleed."

Marceline was still sleeping. We arrived. She had to get out first and saw nothing. Two rooms had been reserved for us. I was able to dash into mine, wash, get rid of the blood. Marceline had seen nothing.

And yet I felt very weak and I had tea sent up for both of us. And while she was preparing it, very calmly, looking a little pale herself, smiling, I felt a kind of irritation because she had been unable to discern anything. I felt as if I were being unfair, it's true; I told myself: "If she saw nothing it's because I was concealing it cleverly." It didn't matter; nothing helped; the feeling welled up in me like an instinct, it overpowered me . . . finally it was too strong; I could no longer control myself; as if casually, I said to her:

"I spat up blood last night."

She didn't call out; she merely became much paler, tottered, tried to hold herself back, and fell heavily onto the floor.

I dashed toward her with a sort of fury: "Marceline! Marceline! — Now look at that! What have I done? Wasn't it enough for *me* to be ill?" But, as I said, I was very weak; I nearly fainted myself. I opened the door; I called; people came to help.

In my suitcase there was, I recalled, a letter of introduction to an officer in the city; on the strength of that note I sent for the medical officer.

Meanwhile Marceline had recovered; now she was beside my bed, in which I was shaking with fever. The medical officer arrived, examined both of us; he assured us that Marceline was perfectly all right and there were no bad effects from her fall; as for me, I was seriously ill; in fact, he refused to give his opinion and he promised to return before evening.

He returned, smiled at me, spoke to me and gave me various medicines. I understood that he thought my case was hopeless. Shall I admit it to you? I wasn't at all startled. I was weary. I merely gave myself up. After all, what did life offer me? I had worked hard up to the end, I had done my duty resolutely and ardently. "As for the rest . . . oh, what does it mean to me?" I thought, finding my stoicism quite noble. But what I was suffering from was the ugliness of that place. "This hotel room is ghastly" — and I looked at it. Suddenly it occurred to me that, just adjacent, in a similar room, was my wife, Marceline; and I heard her talking. The doctor hadn't left; he was conversing with her; he was making an effort to speak low. A little time went by; I had to sleep . . .

When I awoke, Marceline was there. I realized she had been crying. I didn't love life enough to pity myself; but the ugliness of that place irritated me; almost with sensual pleasure, my eyes rested on her.

At the moment, not far from me, she was writing. She looked pretty to me. I saw her seal several letters. Then she stood up, approached my bed and tenderly took my hand.

"How do you feel now?" she said. I smiled, and said sadly: "Will I get better?" But then she replied, "You'll get better!" with such an ardent conviction that, almost convinced myself, I received a kind of confused impression of all that life could be, of her love for me, a vague vision of such touching beauties — that tears flowed from my eyes and I cried for a long time without the power or desire to contain them.

Through enormous strength of love she was able to get me out of Sousse; lovingly cared for, protected, watched over, I journeyed from Sousse to Tunis, then from Tunis to Constantine; Marceline was wonderful. It was at Biskra I was to convalesce. Her confidence was unshakable; her zeal never flagged for a moment. She prepared everything, supervised our departures and made sure of our lodgings. Unfortunately, she couldn't help make the trip less excruciating! Several times I thought I would have to come to a halt and perish. I sweated like a dying man, I choked, at times I blacked out. At the end of the third day, I arrived at Biskra like a dead man.

II

Why speak of the first few days? What is left of them? The terrible memory of them is voiceless. I no longer knew either who or where I was. I merely recall Marceline, my wife, my life, leaning over my death-bed. I know that her fervent care, her love alone, saved me. Finally, one day, just like a lost sailor sighting land, I felt a gleam of life awakening; I had the strength to smile at Marceline. Why recount all this? The important thing is that death had brushed me with its wing, as the saying goes. The important thing is that it became a matter of great surprise to

me to find myself living, that the daylight took on an unexpected brightness for me. Earlier, I thought, I didn't understand that I was living. I
was yet to make the thrilling discovery of life.

A day came when I could get up. I was completely charmed by our
home. It was almost nothing but a terrace, or open gallery. But what a
terrace! My room and Marceline's looked out onto it; it extended over
rooftops. When you reached its highest part, you could see palm trees
rising above the houses; above the palms, the desert. The other side of
the terrace was adjacent to the municipal park; it was shaded by the
branches of the nearest acacias; finally, it ran along the courtyard, a little
regularly shaped courtyard in which were six regularly planted palms,
and it ended at the staircase that joined it to the courtyard. My room
was huge and well ventilated; walls whitewashed, nothing on the walls;
a small door led to Marceline's room; a large glazed door opened onto
the terrace.

There, hourless days flowed by. How often, in my solitude, have
I recalled those slow-moving days! . . . Marceline was beside me. She
read, she sewed, she wrote. I did nothing. I looked at her. Oh,
Marceline! . . . I looked. I saw the sun; I saw the shadow; I saw the line
of shadow moving; I had so little to occupy my mind that I observed it.
I was still very weak; I breathed with difficulty; everything tired me out,
even reading; and, anyway, what was I to read? Just to exist was sufficient
occupation for me.

One morning, Marceline came in laughing:

"I'm bringing a friend for you," she said; and I saw a small, dark-
complexioned Arab boy come in after her. He was called Bashir, he
had large, taciturn eyes that looked at me. I was somewhat annoyed,
on the whole, and that annoyance already fatigued me; I said nothing, I seemed to be angry. The child was confused at the coolness
of my reception; he turned to Marceline and, with a movement of
wheedling animal grace, he snuggled against her, took her hand and
kissed it with a gesture that revealed his bare arms. I noticed that he
was wearing nothing underneath his thin gandurah and his patched
burnoose.°

"Come now! sit down there," Marceline said to him upon seeing my
annoyance. "Play quietly."

The little one sat down on the ground, took a knife out of the hood of

---

° Gandurah: an inner garment, a sleeveless chemise. Burnoose: an outer garment, a
hooded cloak.

his burnoose, then a piece of jerid,* and started to carve it. I thought he wanted to make a whistle.

After a while, I was no longer annoyed by his presence. I looked at him; he seemed to have forgotten he was there. His feet were bare; his ankles were graceful, as were his wrist joints. He handled his poor knife with amusing skill. . . . Was I truly to be interested in that? . . . His hair was shaved in Arab fashion; he was wearing a shabby chéchia† with only a hole where the tassel should be. The gandurah, which had slipped a little, uncovered his dainty shoulder. I felt a need to touch it. I leaned over; he turned around and smiled at me. I signaled to him to hand me his whistle, I took it and pretended to admire it very much. Now he wanted to go. Marceline gave him a pastry, I gave him two sous.

The next day, for the first time, I was bored; I waited; waited for what? I felt unoccupied, restless. Finally I could no longer stand it:

"Well, isn't Bashir coming this morning?"

"If you like, I'll go find him."

She left me, went downstairs; after a moment she returned alone. What had my sickness done to me? I was so sad to see her come back without Bashir that I felt like crying.

"It was too late," she told me; "the children have left school and have scattered everywhere. There are charming ones, you know. I think they all know me by now."

"Anyway, try to get him here tomorrow."

The next day Bashir returned. He sat down as he had two days earlier, took out his knife and, attempting to carve a piece of wood that was too hard, finally plunged the blade into his thumb. I shuddered with horror; he laughed at it, showed me the shining cut and enjoyed watching his blood flow. Whenever he laughed, he revealed very white teeth; he licked his wound amusingly; his tongue was pink as a cat's. Oh, how fit he was! That was what caught my fancy in him: his good health. The healthiness of that little body was beautiful.

The next day he brought along marbles. He wanted me to play. Marceline wasn't there; she would have forbidden it. I hesitated, I looked at Bashir; the boy grabbed my arm, put the marbles into my hand, forced me. Stooping down put me considerably out of breath, but I tried to play all the same. Finally I was no longer able to. I was soaked with sweat. I tossed aside the marbles and dropped into an armchair. Bashir, a little worried, was looking at me.

---

* A palm stalk stripped of its leaves.
† A cylindrical skullcap.

"Sick?" he said politely; the tone of his voice was exquisite. Marceline came home.

"Take him away," I said to her; "I'm tired this morning."

A few hours later I spat blood. It was while I was walking painfully on the terrace; Marceline was busy in her room; fortunately she couldn't see anything. From shortness of breath, I had inhaled too deeply, and suddenly it was upon me. It filled my mouth. . . . But it was no longer fresh blood, as with the first expectorations; it was a horrible large clot that I spat out onto the ground in disgust.

I took a few steps, staggering. I was terribly worked up. I was trembling. I was afraid; I was furious. For up until then I had thought I was going to get better little by little, and that all I had to do was wait. This unforeseen occurrence had just set me back. Oddly enough, the first expectorations hadn't affected me that badly; I now recalled that they had left me nearly calm. Then, why was I so afraid and terrified now? Because, unfortunately, I was beginning to love life.

I walked back, stooped down, found what I had spat out, took a straw and, lifting the clot, put it on my handkerchief. I looked at it. It was ugly, almost black, blood, something sticky, frightful . . . I thought about Bashir's beautiful, gleaming blood . . . And suddenly I was seized by a desire, a wish, something more rabid, more imperious, than anything I had felt until then: to live! I wanted to live. I wanted to live. I clenched my teeth and my fists, I concentrated entirely, desperately, desolately, on that effort to go on existing.

The day before I had received a letter from T.; in reply to anxious questions from Marceline, it was full of medical advice; T. had even enclosed in his letter a few medical pamphlets written for a general audience, as well as a more technical book, which therefore seemed more serious to me. I had read the letter carelessly and hadn't read the printed matter at all; first, because the resemblance of those pamphlets to the little treatises on morality with which my childhood had been plagued made them unwelcome to me; and also because all advice bothered me; besides, I didn't think that titles like "Advice to the Tubercular" or "Practical Tubercular Care" could be applicable to my case. I didn't think I had tuberculosis. I liked to think that my first blood spitting had a different cause; or, rather, to tell the truth, I didn't search for any cause, I avoided thinking about it, I rarely thought about it, and I considered myself, if not cured, at least close to it. . . . I read the letter. I devoured the book and the pamphlets. Suddenly, with frightening obviousness, it was clear to me that I hadn't been taking proper care of myself. Up to then I had just gone on living, trusting in the vaguest hope. Suddenly I saw that my life was being attacked, horribly attacked at its very core. A host of active enemies were living inside me. I listened to them; I was on the alert for them; I felt them. I wouldn't overcome them without a struggle . . . and I added, in a low voice, as if to convince myself of it further: "It's a matter of willpower."

I prepared myself for war.

Evening was falling; I planned my strategy. For a while, I was to concentrate on nothing but getting better; my health was my first duty; I had to consider as good, to deem correct, everything that was beneficial to me, to forget and reject everything that did not contribute to the cure. Before the evening meal, I had made resolutions concerning my breathing, exercise and eating habits.

We took our meals in a sort of little kiosk surrounded on all sides by the terrace. Alone, at peace, far from the world, we treasured the intimacy of our meals. An old black man brought us tolerable food from a nearby hotel. Marceline reviewed the menus, ordered one dish, vetoed another. . . . Not being very hungry for the most part, I didn't mind too much if a dish was badly cooked or if the meal was scanty. Marceline, herself accustomed to not eating much, didn't know or realize that I wasn't getting enough to eat. To eat a lot was the first of all my resolutions. I intended to put it into effect that very evening. I couldn't. We had some kind of uneatable ragout, then a roast that was ridiculously overcooked.

I was so irritated that I took it out on Marceline, letting out my heart in unguarded terms. I accused her; to hear me, it seemed that she should have felt responsible for the bad quality of that food. That slight delay in adopting the diet I had resolved on assumed the gravest importance; I forgot about the days before; this bad meal ruined everything. I became obstinate. Marceline had to go down into town to look for canned food, any kind of pâté.

She soon returned with a small terrine, which I gobbled up almost completely, as if to prove to both of us how great my need was to eat more.

That very evening we made this decision: The meals would be much better; more frequent, too, one every three hours, the first of the day as early as six-thirty. A large supply of all kinds of canned food would supplement the mediocre dishes from the hotel. . . .

I couldn't sleep that night, I was so giddy with the foretaste of my newfound virtues. I think I had some fever; a bottle of mineral water was there beside me; I drank a glass of it, two glasses; the third time, drinking right from the bottle, I finished it all at once. I reviewed my willpower plan like a school lesson; I became aware of my hostility and directed it against everything; I had to combat everything: my deliverance depended on myself alone.

Finally I saw the night grow pallid; day appeared.

That had been my vigil of arms.*

The next day was Sunday. Until then, I must admit, I hadn't been concerned about Marceline's religious beliefs; out of indifference or reserve, I felt they were no concern of mine; besides, I attached no importance to them. That day Marceline went to Mass. When she returned I learned that she had prayed for me. I stared at her, then said, with all the gentleness I could muster:

"You mustn't pray for me, Marceline."

"Why not?" she said, a little upset.

"I don't like being protected."

"You reject the aid of God?"

"Later on, He'd have a claim to my gratitude. That creates obligations; I don't want any."

We seemed to be joking, but we weren't deceived about the gravity of our words.

"My poor husband, you'll never get better all on your own," she sighed.

"In that case, too bad about it . . ." Then, seeing her sadness, I added, less brutally: "*You* will help me."

III

I'm going to talk for quite some time about my body. I'm going to talk about it so much, you'll think at first that I'm forgetting the role of the mind. In this narrative, the oversight is intentional; then and there, it was real. I did not yet have enough strength to lead a double life. "My mind and all that," I said to myself, "I'll think about them later on, when I feel better."

I was still far from feeling good. For any trifle, I broke into a sweat and for any trifle I caught a chill; I had what Rousseau called "short breath"; sometimes a little fever; often, from the morning on, a feeling of terrible lassitude, and, at those times, I remained sprawling in

---

* Historically, a night spent awake before being accepted into knighthood.

an armchair, indifferent to everything, self-centered, paying attention to nothing whatever except trying to breathe properly. I would breathe laboriously, methodically, carefully; I would exhale in two sharp jerks, which my overstrained willpower couldn't completely subdue; even for a long time afterward, I avoided them only by dint of strict attention.

But what I suffered from most was my sickly sensitivity to any change in temperature. When I reflect on it today, I think a generalized nervous complaint was added to my illness; I can't explain in any other way a series of phenomena that don't strike me as an essential part of the tubercular condition. I was always either too hot or too cold; I covered myself up at once, overdoing it ridiculously; I would no sooner stop shivering than I was sweating; I would uncover myself a bit and would start shivering the moment I was no longer sweating. Parts of my body became chilled; in spite of the sweat, they became as cold to the touch as a block of marble; nothing could warm them up again. I was so sensitive to cold that a little water spilling onto my foot when I was washing up gave me a head cold; and equally sensitive to heat. . . . I retained that sensitivity, I still retain it, but today in order to derive sensual pleasure from it. Any intense sensitivity, I think, depending on whether the organism is robust or feeble, can become the cause of enjoyment or discomfort. Everything that disturbed me in the past has become delightful to me.

I don't know how I had managed up till then to sleep with my windows closed; therefore, on T.'s advice, I tried opening them at night; at first, only slightly; soon I opened them all the way; soon it was a habit, a need so great that the moment the window was closed again I was stifled. With what delight, later on, I was to feel the night breeze and the moonlight entering my room. . . .

I can't wait by now to come to an end of these first stammerings of restored health. In fact, thanks to constant care, the fresh air, the best nourishment, it wasn't long before I felt better. Up to that time, afraid of running out of breath on the staircase, I hadn't dared to leave the terrace; finally, during the last days of January, I went down and ventured into the park.

Marceline was accompanying me, carrying a shawl. It was three in the afternoon. The wind, which is often strong in that region and had been bothering me badly for three days, had dropped. The air was delightfully mild.

The public park . . . it is traversed by a very wide walk shaded by two rows of that very tall variety of mimosa locally called acacias. Benches are located in the shade of those trees. A stream that is canalized — I mean it is more deep than wide, and nearly straight — flows alongside the walk; then other, smaller canals divide the water of the stream, leading it across the garden toward the plants; the sluggish water is earth-colored, the color of pink or gray clay. Almost no foreigners, a few Arabs; they walk around and, as soon as they move out of the sunlight, their white capes take on the color of the shade.

An odd shudder came over me when I entered that strange shade; I wrapped myself up in my shawl; yet I felt no discomfort; just the opposite. . . . We sat down on a bench. Marceline was silent. Arabs went by; then a troop of children arrived. Marceline knew some of them and beckoned to them; they came over. She told me some of their names; there were questions, answers, frowns, little games. All of that annoyed me to some extent and my discomfort returned; I felt tired and sweaty. But, I must admit, what bothered me wasn't the children, it was her. Yes, though ever so slightly, I was bothered by her presence. If I had stood up, she would have followed me; if I had taken off my shawl, she would have wanted to carry it; if I had then put it back on again, she would have said, "You're not cold, are you?" Besides, I didn't dare talk to the children in front of her; I saw that she had her favorites; in spite of myself, yet intentionally, I took interest in the others. "Let's go back in," I said to her; and I made a secret resolve to return to the park alone.

The next day, she had to go out about ten; I took advantage of that. Little Bashir, who rarely failed to come in the morning, took my shawl; I felt alert, lighthearted. We were almost alone on the park path; I would walk slowly, sit down for a moment and start out again. Bashir followed me, chattering, faithful and pliant as a dog. I arrived at the spot on the canal where the washerwomen come to wash; in the middle of the current a flat stone is laid; on it a little girl, lying down with her face leaning over the water, her hand in the current, was throwing tiny twigs into it or fishing them out. Her bare feet had been thrust into the water; from that immersion they had retained a trace of moisture, and her skin looked darker in that area. Bashir went up to her and spoke to her; she turned around, smiled at me, and answered Bashir in Arabic. "She's my sister," he told me; then he explained to me that his mother was going to come and wash clothes, and that his little sister was waiting for her. Her name was Rhadra, which meant "green" in Arabic. He said all this in a delightful, bright voice as childlike as the emotion it afforded me.

"She asks you to give her two sous," he added.

I gave her ten and was preparing to leave when his mother, the washerwoman, arrived. She was an admirable woman, statuesque, her wide forehead tattooed in blue; she was carrying a basket of clothes on her head like the canephorae* of antiquity and, like them, she was draped in simple fashion in a wide, dark blue garment tucked up at the waist and falling in a straight line down to the feet. As soon as she saw Bashir, she scolded him harshly. He replied violently; the little girl joined in; an extremely lively argument ensued among the three of them. Finally Bashir, as if vanquished, gave me to understand that his mother needed him that morning; he handed me my shawl sadly and I had to leave all by myself.

I hadn't taken twenty steps before my shawl seemed unbearably heavy to me; soaked in sweat, I sat down on the first bench I found. I was hoping that a child would come along who would relieve me of that burden. The one who arrived before long was a tall boy of fourteen, black as a Sudanese, not at all shy, who spontaneously offered his services. His name was Ashur. He would have struck me as handsome except that he was blind in one eye. He liked to chat, told me where the stream came from, and informed me that after exiting the park it flowed into the oasis, which it crossed in its entirety. I listened to him, forgetting my fatigue. However pleasant Bashir seemed to me, I knew him too well by this time and I was glad of the change. In fact, I promised myself that, another day, I would come down to the garden all alone, sit on a bench and wait for the chance of a felicitous meeting. . . .

After I had stopped for several moments more, Ashur and I arrived in front of my door. I wanted to invite him up, but didn't dare to, not knowing what Marceline would have thought of it.

I found her in the dining room taking care of a very young child, so puny and stunted-looking that at first I felt more disgust than pity for him. A little timorously, Marceline said to me:

"This poor little one is sick."

"I hope it isn't contagious. What's wrong with him?"

"I don't know yet exactly. He says he hurts a little bit all over. His French is very poor; when Bashir is here tomorrow, he can act as his interpreter. . . . I'm making him drink a little tea. . . ."

Then, as if to apologize, and because I was standing there saying nothing, she added: "I've known him for some time now; up to now I didn't dare have him come here; I was afraid of tiring you, or perhaps displeasing you."

"Why?" I cried out. "Bring all the children here you want, if that entertains you!" And, a bit annoyed that I hadn't done so, I thought that I could just as well have asked Ashur up.

---

* Women carrying baskets in ancient Greek ceremonies.

Meanwhile I was looking at my wife; she was maternal and affectionate. Her tenderness was so touching that the little one soon left feeling quite comforted. I spoke about my outing and, without being unkind about it, explained to Marceline why I preferred going out alone.

My nights were generally still punctuated by startled awakenings, when I would either feel chilled or be dripping with sweat. This night was very placid and I awoke very infrequently. The next morning I was ready to go out by nine. The weather was fine; I felt well rested, not at all weak; I was cheerful or, rather, amused. The air was still and tepid, but I took my shawl anyway, as a pretext for making the acquaintance of whoever would carry it for me. I have said that the park was adjacent to our terrace; I therefore went there at once. I entered its shade with delight. The air was luminous. The acacias, which have flowers that appear very early, before their leaves, were fragrant — unless that sort of light aroma, which seemed to enter me through several senses at once, and which was exciting me, came from everywhere. Moreover, I was breathing more easily, which made it easier for me to walk; and yet, at the first bench I came to I sat down, but more tipsy, more befuddled, than weary. I looked around. The shade was in motion and weightless; it wasn't falling onto the ground, and seemed barely to rest there. O light! I listened. What did I hear? Nothing; everything; I was enchanted by every sound. I remember a bush whose bark, from a distance, seemed to have such a peculiar texture that I had to get up and go feel it. I touched it as if caressing it; I experienced a thrill of delight. I remember . . . Was it on that morning that I was finally to be reborn?

I had forgotten that I was alone, I was awaiting nothing, I forgot the time. It seemed to me that until that day I had felt so little, and instead thought so much, that I was finally surprised by this: my power to feel was becoming as strong as my power of thought.

I say "it seemed to me" — because, from the remotest nooks of the past, from my earliest childhood, a thousand glimmerings were at last awakening, aroused by a thousand forgotten sensations. The new realization of my senses that I was gaining allowed me to review these memories uneasily. Yes, my senses, from now on completely awake, were discovering that they had an entire history, they were recreating their own past. They were alive! They were alive! They had never ceased to live, they were finding that, even through my years of studies, they had led a latent, clandestine life.

I made no acquaintances that day, and I was glad of it; I took from my pocket a little volume of Homer that I hadn't reopened since my departure from Marseilles; I reread three lines of the Odyssey, memorized them, then, finding sufficient nourishment in their rhythm and delighting in them at my leisure, I closed the book and remained there trembling, more alive than I would have thought anyone could be, and with my mind numbed by happiness. . . .

IV

Meanwhile, Marceline, who was overjoyed to see my health finally restored, had begun a few days earlier to tell me about the wonderful orchards in the oasis.* She loved the outdoors and walking. The freedom afforded her by my illness allowed her to make long jaunts, from which she came back dazzled; up to this point, she had hardly spoken about them, feeling it unsafe to encourage me to accompany her, and fearing to see me saddened by accounts of pleasures that I could not yet enjoy. But, now that I was feeling better, she counted on their appeal to put me back on my feet altogether. The satisfaction I was rediscovering in walking and observing things inclined me that way. And the very next day we set out together.

She walked ahead of me on an odd path such as I had never seen in any country. It meanders as if indolently between two quite high earthen walls; the shapes of the gardens bounded by these high walls incline it as they will; it curves or sets off at a new angle; as soon as you enter it, you get lost in a turning; you no longer know where you've come from or where you're going. The faithful waters of the stream follow the path alongside one of the walls; the walls are formed of the very earth of the road, that of the whole oasis, a pinkish or soft gray clay which the water makes a little darker, which the burning sun cracks, and which hardens in the heat but softens at the first shower, when it creates a yielding surface that retains the imprints of one's bare feet. Above the walls, palm trees. As we approached, turtle-doves flew into them. Marceline was looking at me.

I was forgetting my weariness and discomfort. I was walking in a kind of rapture, a silent cheerfulness, a heightening of the senses and the flesh. At that moment, light breezes arose; all the palm leaves shook and

---

* Date palms and fruit trees grow in the Biskra oasis.

we saw the tallest of the trees bend. Then the air became completely calm, and from behind the wall I distinctly heard the melody of a flute. A breach in the wall; we went in.

It was a spot full of shade and light; tranquil and seemingly sheltered from the weather; full of silence and rustling, the light sound of water flowing, watering the palms and running from tree to tree; the quiet call of the turtle-doves, the melody of a flute that a child was playing. He was tending a flock of goats; he was seated, all but naked, on the trunk of a fallen palm; he was not disturbed at our approach, didn't run away, interrupted his playing for only a moment.

During that short silence I noticed that another flute was answering in the distance. We moved a little closer, then Marceline said: "It's pointless to go any farther; these orchards are all alike; they merely get slightly more extensive at the far end of the oasis. . . ." She spread out the shawl on the ground, saying: "Take a rest."

How long did we stay there? I can't recall — what difference did the time make? Marceline was near me; I stretched out, resting my head on her knees. The flute melody continued to flow, stopped occasionally, resumed; the sound of the water . . . From time to time a goat would bleat. I closed my eyes; I felt Marceline's cool hand resting on my forehead; I felt the burning sunshine gently filtered through the palm leaves; I wasn't thinking of a thing; what did thinking matter? My feelings were amazingly strong. . . .

And, from time to time, a new sound; I would open my eyes; it was the light breeze in the palm leaves; it didn't come all the way down to where we were, it stirred only the palm leaves high up. . . .

The next morning, I returned to the same garden with Marceline; on the evening of that same day I went there alone. The flute-playing goatherd was there. I went up to him and spoke to him. His name was Lassif, he was only twelve, he was good-looking. He told me the names of his goats, told me that the canals are called seghias; not all of them flow every day, he informed me; the water, distributed wisely and frugally, quenches the thirst of the plants and is then immediately withdrawn from them. At the foot of each palm tree a narrow tank is dug that contains the water to irrigate the tree; an ingenious system of sluices, which the child explained to me by putting them into action, controls the water, leading it where the thirst is excessive.

The next day I saw a brother of Lassif: he was a little older, less good-looking; his name was Lashmi. By means of a kind of ladder formed along the trunk by the scars of the leaves cut in the past, he climbed to the very top of a pollarded palm; then he descended nimbly, exhibiting his gilded skin beneath his waving cape. From the top of the tree, the tip of which had been sliced away, he brought a small earthen gourd; it was hung up there, near the recent wound, to gather the palm sap, from which is made a sweet wine that the Arabs prize. At Lashmi's invitation I sampled it; but I didn't like that insipid, tart, syrupy taste.

On the days that followed I took longer walks; I saw other gardens, other shepherds and other goats. As Marceline had said, those gardens were all alike; and yet each one had something different.

Sometimes Marceline would still accompany me; but, more often, as soon as we got to the orchards, I would leave her, persuading her that I was weary, that I wanted to sit down, that she shouldn't wait for me because she needed to go on walking; and so she would finish her stroll without me. I would stay with the children. Soon I had met a large number of them; I would chat with them for long periods; I learned their games, showed them others, and lost all my sous at the game of corks.* Some of the children accompanied me for a good distance (every day I was walking farther); they would show me a new passageway home and they would carry my coat and shawl for me when I occasionally took them both off; before leaving them I would give out small coins; sometimes, still playing, they followed me all the way to my door; finally, they sometimes passed through it.

Then Marceline, for her part, brought others. She would bring the ones from the school, whom she encouraged to work hard; when classes were over, the well-behaved and mild-mannered ones would come upstairs; the ones I would bring were different; but they would get together at games. We made sure we always had syrups and candies ready. Soon others came of their own accord, even ones we hadn't invited. I recall each one of them; I can still see them. . . .

Toward the end of January, the weather suddenly turned bad; a cold wind started to blow and my health was immediately affected. The great open space separating the oasis from the town became unbridgeable for me again, and once more I had to be satisfied with the public park. Then it rained; an icy rain, which on the edge of the horizon, in the north, covered the mountains with snow.

I spent those sad days near the fire, gloomy, fighting furiously against the illness, which, in that bad weather, was triumphant. Mournful days:

---

* The purpose of this game was to throw quoits or other objects to knock over corks that had coins on them.

I could neither read nor work; the least effort brought on uncomfortable sweating; it was exhausting to concentrate my attention; whenever I wasn't careful about breathing properly, I would choke.

The children, during those sad days, were the only distraction possible for me. Only the most familiar ones would venture to come in the rain; their clothes were soaked; they would sit down in front of the fire, in a circle. Long moments went by without conversation. I was too tired, too ill, to do anything but look at them; but their healthy presence was good for me. Those whom Marceline made much of were weak, puny and too well behaved; I was annoyed with her and them, and finally rejected them. To tell the truth, they frightened me.

One morning I made a curious discovery about myself: Moktir, the only one of my wife's favorites who didn't annoy me at all (maybe because he was good-looking), was alone with me in my room; up to then I had liked him only moderately, but now his gleaming dark eyes intrigued me. A curiosity I couldn't exactly explain to myself caused me to observe his gestures. I was standing near the fire, my two elbows on the mantel, in front of a book, and I appeared to be absorbed, but I could see reflected in the mirror the movements of the child, to whom I had my back turned. Moktir didn't know he was being watched and thought I was deep in my book. I saw him noiselessly approach a table on which, next to a piece of needlework, Marceline had placed a small pair of scissors, which he seized furtively and thrust into his burnoose all at once. For an instant my heart pounded, but the wisest reasoning failed to induce in me the slightest feeling of repugnance. What's more, I couldn't manage to convince myself that the feeling which then overcame me was anything but joy. After I had allowed Moktir all the time he needed to do a good job of robbing me, I turned toward him again and spoke to him as if nothing had happened. Marceline liked that child very much; and yet, when I saw her next, I don't think it was the fear of hurting her that made me invent some yarn or other to explain the loss of the scissors, rather than accuse Moktir. From that day on, Moktir became my favorite.

V

Our stay at Biskra was not to last much longer. Once the February rains had ended, the heat that broke out was too strong. After several painful days, which we had lived through under showers, suddenly one morning I awoke in the midst of the blue. As soon as I got up I ran to the highest level of the terrace. From one end of the horizon to the other, the sky was clear. Beneath the sun, already blazing, vapors were rising; the whole oasis was smoking; in the distance you could hear the rumbling of the overflowing wadi.* The air was so fresh and beautiful that I immediately felt better. Marceline came; we wanted to go out, but that day we were kept in by the mud.

A few days later we were returning to Lassif's orchard; the plant stalks seemed heavy, soft and waterlogged. That African soil, with whose powers of expectancy I was unfamiliar, had been drenched for long days, and was now awakening from winter, intoxicated with water, bursting with new sap; it was smiling with a frantic springtime, of which I felt the reverberations and, as it were, the counterpart in myself. Ashur and Moktir accompanied us at first; I was still fond of their unburdensome friendship that cost only half a franc per day; but soon, tired of them, no longer being so weak myself that I still needed the example of their good health, and no longer finding in their games the nourishment necessary for my happiness, I transferred to Marceline the excitement of my mind and senses. From the happiness this gave her I realized that earlier she had remained sad. I apologized like a child for having frequently abandoned her, I blamed my weakness for my changeable and peculiar moods, I asserted that up until then I had been too weary to be a lover, but that from here on I would feel my love increasing as my health improved. I was telling the truth; but I was surely still very weak, because it still took more than a month for me to feel a desire for Marceline.

Meanwhile, the heat was increasing daily. There was nothing to keep us in Biskra — except the charm that was to draw me back there again. Our decision to leave was a sudden one. Within three hours we had finished packing. The train was to leave the next day at dawn. . . .

I remember the last night. The moon was nearly full; through my wide-open window it flooded my room. Marceline was sleeping, I think. I was in bed, but unable to sleep. I felt burned up by a kind of happy fever, which was nothing else than life. . . . I got up, dipped my hands and face into water, then, pushing the glass door, I went out.

It was already late; not a sound; not a breath; even the air seemed to

---

* Like a North American arroyo, a wadi is a stream in hot, dry regions that can become completely dry in summer and torrential in the rainy season. The particular wadi in question here is called the Oued Biskra.

be asleep. Barely, in the distance, could be heard the Arabs' dogs, which yap like jackals all night long. In front of me, the little courtyard; the wall opposite me cast a slanting path of shadow onto it; the regularly planted palms, without any more color or life, seemed forever immobilized. . . . But in sleep you can still detect a throb of life — here nothing seemed asleep; everything seemed dead. I took fright at that calm; and suddenly I was once more overcome — like a protest, an affirmation and a despair in the silence — by the tragic sense of my life: so violently, almost painfully, and so impetuously that it would have made me cry out, had I been able to cry out as animals do. I placed my hand, I remember — my left hand, into my right; I wanted to raise it to my head, and I did so. Why? To assure myself that I was alive, and to find that remarkable. I touched my forehead, my eyelids. A shiver ran through me. "A day will come," I thought, "a day will come when I won't have enough strength even to raise to my lips the very water I will thirst for. . . ." I went back in but did not yet go back to bed; I wanted to make that night indelible, to impress the memory of it upon my mind, to hold onto it; not sure of what I would do, I picked up a book from my table — the Bible — and let it open at random; leaning over it in the moonlight, I could read it; I read those words spoken by Christ to Peter, those words I was unfortunately never to forget again: "When thou wast young, thou girdedst thyself, and walkedst whither thou wouldest; but when thou shalt be old, thou shalt stretch forth thy hands. . . ."* Thou shalt stretch forth thy hands . . .

The next day, at dawn, we departed.

VI

I won't talk about each stage of the journey. Some of them left only a confused memory; my health, now better and now worse, still tottered in a cold wind, was still dismayed by the shadow of a cloud, and the state of my nerves produced frequent agitations; but at least my lungs were healing. Each relapse was less protracted and less serious; the onset was just as drastic, but my body was gaining better defenses against it.

From Tunis we had gone to Malta, then to Syracuse; I was returning to the classic soil whose language and history were well known to

---

* St. John 21:18.

me. Since the beginning of my illness, I had lived without scrutinizing myself or obeying any law, merely attempting to live, in the manner of animals or children. Now that I was less absorbed by the disease, my life became steadfast and self-conscious again. After that long agony, I had thought I had been reborn as the same man, that I could soon link up my present to my past; amid the strangeness of an unknown land I was able to deceive myself in that way; here, no longer; all things informed me of a fact that still surprised me: I had changed.

When, in Syracuse and later on, I tried to resume my studies, to immerse myself as I used to in the detailed investigation of history, I discovered that something had, if not destroyed, at least altered, its savor for me; it was the sense of the present. The history of the past now took on in my eyes that immobility, that frightening rigidity of the nighttime shadows in the little courtyard at Biskra, the immobility of death. Earlier, I had been pleased by that very rigidity, which allowed my mind to operate with precision; all the data of history seemed to me like the exhibits in a museum or, rather, like the plants in a herbarium, whose permanent dried-out state could help me forget that one day, rich with sap, they had lived beneath the sun. Now, if I could still take pleasure in history, it was by imagining that it was taking place in the present. Thus, the major political events were to stir me much less than the emotion now reviving within me for the poets or for certain men of action. At Syracuse I reread Theocritus,* and it occurred to me that his shepherds, with their beautiful names, were the very ones whom I had loved at Biskra.

My scholarship, which was awakening at each step I took, became a burden to me, obstructing my happiness. I couldn't look at a Greek theater, a temple, without immediately reconstructing it mentally. For each ancient festival, the ruins that remained in its place made me sorrowful at its demise; and I was horrified by death.

Soon I shunned ruins, and preferred to the loveliest monuments of the past those low gardens called the *latomie*, where the lemons have the acid sweetness of oranges, and the banks of the Ciane, which, amid the papyrus, still flows as blue as on the days when it did so to mourn Proserpina.†

---

* The foremost Greek pastoral poet, 3rd century B.C., a native of Syracuse.
† The *latomie* are ancient stone quarries, now public parks. Proserpina is the Latin form of Persephone, the earth goddess' daughter abducted by the ruler of the underworld to become his consort. Grief over the abduction caused the nymph Cyane to be transformed into a spring.

I came to despise in myself that knowledge of which at first I was so proud; those studies, which at first meant my whole life, no longer seemed to have anything more than a quite accidental and conventional relationship to me. I was finding myself a different person and, to my joy, I had an existence outside them. As an expert, I felt stupid. As a man, did I know myself? I was only at the point of being born and I could not yet know who this new-born self was. That is what I had to learn.

There is nothing more tragic, for a man who thought he was dying, than a slow convalescence. After the wing of death has brushed you, what used to seem important is so no longer; other things are instead, things that didn't formerly seem important or that you didn't even know existed. The accumulation of all acquired knowledge in our mind flakes away like a cosmetic and in places lets us see the bare flesh, the authentic being that was hidden.

From then on, *that* was whom I strove to discover: my authentic self, the "old Adam," the one rejected by the Gospels; the man whom everything around me, books, teachers, relatives and I myself, had tried at first to suppress. And, because of those additional burdens, he already seemed to me more blurred and harder to find, but all the more useful to find and valorous. From then on, I despised that secondary, acquired self superimposed by my education. I had to shake off those burdens.

And I compared myself to palimpsests: I shared the joy of the scholar who discovers, beneath more recent writing, a very old, infinitely more valuable, text on the same sheet of paper. What was this obscured text? To read it, wasn't it first necessary to erase the recent texts?

And so I was no longer the sickly, studious being for whom my previous set of morals, so rigid and confining, had been suitable. More than a convalescence was in progress here; it was a growth, a resurgence of life, an influx of richer, warmer blood that was to affect my thoughts, affect them one by one, to penetrate everything, to stir and color the most remote, delicate and secret fibers of my being. For one becomes accustomed to sturdiness or weakness; one's being shapes itself in accordance with the strength at its disposal; but let that strength increase, let it permit greater capabilities, and . . . I didn't have all these thoughts at that time, and my depiction here falsifies the situation. To tell the truth, I wasn't thinking or examining myself at all; a felicitous fate was guiding me. I feared that a too hasty glance might disturb the mystery of my slow transformation. I had to give the obscured writing enough time to reappear, it was wrong to reconstitute it too eagerly. Thus, allowing

my brain, not to drift aimlessly, but to lie fallow, I voluptuously dedicated myself to my own being, to the objects around me, to the universe,
which seemed godlike to me. We had left Syracuse and I was running along the precipitous road that links Taormina with Castel Mola,*
shouting, in order to summon it to me: "A new being! A new being!"

Therefore, my sole effort — a constant effort at that time — was to
vilify or eliminate systematically everything I believed I owed only to
my past education and childhood morals. Out of a resolute contempt
for my knowledge, out of scorn for my scholarly tastes, I refused to see
Agrigento, and, a few days later, on the road to Naples, I didn't stop at
the beautiful temple† of Paestum, where the spirit of Greece still survives
and which I visited two years later in order to pray to some god, I've
forgotten which.

Why do I speak of a sole effort? Could I have an interest in myself unless I thought I was a being capable of perfection? That unknown perfection, which I then imagined so vaguely — my willpower had never been
so intense as it now was to attain it; I used every bit of that willpower to
strengthen my body, to harden it. Near Salerno, leaving the coast, we
had reached Ravello. There, the keener air, the attraction of the crags
full of recesses and surprises, the unknown depth of the ravines, aiding
my strength and my joy, favored my zeal.

Closer to the sky than it is distant from the shore, Ravello, on an
abrupt height, faces the far-off, flat strand at Paestum. Under Norman
rule, it was nearly a large city; it is now merely a huddled village, in
which I think we were the only foreigners. A former religious house,
now converted into a hotel, sheltered us; located at the edge of the
crag, its terraces and garden seemed to overhang the blue sky. After the
grapevine-laden wall, nothing could be seen at first but the sea; you had
to approach the wall to discern the cultivated slopes that, by stairways
rather than paths, joined Ravello to the shore. Above Ravello, the mountain range continued. Olive trees, enormous carob trees; in their shade,
cyclamens; higher up, chestnut trees in great number, cool air, northern
plants; lower down, lemon trees near the sea. They are aligned in small
groves dictated by the slope of the soil; they are stepped orchards, almost
all alike; a narrow walk, in their midst, crosses them from one end to
another; you enter them noiselessly, like a thief. You dream beneath that
green shade; the foliage is dense, heavy; not one clear sunbeam pierces
it; like drops of thick wax the fragrant lemons hang; in the shade they

---

* A village on a high, rocky spur overlooking Taormina.
† There are actually several.

are white and greenish; they are within reach of your hand, your thirst; they are sweet and tart; they refresh you.

The shade was so total, beneath them, that I didn't dare stop there after walking, which still made me sweat. And yet the stairlike ascent no longer tired me out; I practiced walking up with my mouth closed; I made my pauses less and less frequent, telling myself: "I'll go up to that point without feeling weak"; then, having reached my goal and feeling rewarded by my satisfied pride, I would breathe strongly for some time, in such a way that I seemed to feel the air penetrating my chest more effectually. I transferred my former diligence to all those bodily concerns. I was making progress.

Sometimes I was surprised at how quickly my health was returning. I came to believe that I had at first exaggerated the seriousness of my condition, to doubt that I had been very ill, to laugh at the blood I had spat up, to regret that my cure hadn't been more arduous.

At first I had taken very bad care of myself, unaware of my body's needs. I studied these patiently and, as far as caution and care go, I developed such a constant ingeniousness that it entertained me like a game. What I still suffered from most was my sickly sensitivity to the slightest change in temperature. Now that my lungs were cured, I attributed this supersensitivity to my frayed nerves, an aftereffect of the illness. I determined to overcome that. The sight of the beautiful tanned and, one could say, sun-drenched skins displayed by some disarrayed rustics, as they worked in the fields with open jackets, encouraged me to get a tan as well. One morning, I stripped and observed myself; the sight of my overly thin arms, of my shoulders which, with the greatest efforts, I failed to throw back sufficiently, but especially the whiteness or, rather, the bleaching-out of my skin, filled me with both shame and tears. I dressed again quickly and, instead of walking down toward Amalfi, as I had grown used to doing, I directed my steps toward rocks covered with low grass and moss, far from dwellings, far from roads, where I knew I couldn't be seen. Once there, I slowly undressed. The air was nearly brisk, but the sun was blazing. I offered my whole body to its flame. I sat, I stretched out, I turned. I felt the hard earth beneath me; the waving wild grasses brushed me. Although sheltered from the wind, I shivered and throbbed at each gust. Soon I was enveloped by a delightful warmth; my whole being was concentrated in my skin.

We stayed in Ravello two weeks; every morning I went back to those rocks and took a treatment. Soon the excess clothing I was still wearing became annoying and unnecessary; my invigorated skin stopped sweating endlessly and became able to protect itself with its own warmth.

On the morning of one of the final days (it was mid-April) I became more adventurous. In a cleft among the rocks I have been speaking of there flowed a clear spring. At this spot it even formed a waterfall, not of great volume, it's true, but below the fall it had dug out a rather deep pool where the very pure water lingered. Three times I had come, had bent over it, had stretched out on the edge, full of thirst and full of desires; I had observed for long periods the bottom of the pool, formed of polished stone, where not a stain, not a blade of grass was to be seen, where the sun penetrated, vibrating and breaking into patterns. On that fourth day, having made my resolve in advance, I went right up to that water, which was clearer than ever, and, without reflecting further, I dived in all at once. Feeling chilled quickly, I left the water and stretched out on the grass, in the sunshine. There, aromatic mints were growing; I picked some, I crushed their leaves and with them I rubbed my whole moist but burning body. I observed myself for some time, without any more shame, with joy. I found myself, not yet robust, but with the possibility of becoming robust, I found myself harmonious, sensual, almost beautiful.

VII

And so, for all activity, for all labor, I was contenting myself with physical exercises that, of course, implied a change in my moral values, but by now seemed to me merely a course of training, a means toward an end, and no longer satisfied me in themselves.

Yet, I performed another act, which you may find laughable but which I shall report to you, because in its very childishness it defines the need, then tormenting me, to manifest outwardly the inner change in my nature: at Amalfi, I had had myself shaved clean.

Up to that day I had worn a full beard, and my hair clipped very close. It never occurred to me that I could just as well have sported a different style. And suddenly, the day that I first lay naked on that rock, that beard bothered me; it was like a final garment of which I couldn't rid myself; I felt it to be like an artificial appendage; it was carefully cut, not into a point but into a square shape that immediately struck me as being very unpleasing and ridiculous. Back in my hotel room I looked at myself in the mirror and didn't like myself; I looked like what I had been up to then: a student of palaeography. Right after lunch, I went down to

Amalfi, my mind made up. The town is very small: I had to be satisfied with a common stall in the main square. It was a market day; the shop was full; I had to wait endlessly; but nothing — not the dubious razors, the yellow brush, the smell, the barber's conversation — could make me back down. Feeling my beard falling away beneath the scissors, I felt as if I were removing a mask. No matter! When I looked at myself afterward, the emotion that filled me, and which I repressed as best I could, was not joy but fear. I am not disputing that feeling, merely reporting it. I found my features handsome enough . . . no, the fear came from my notion that my thoughts could be seen in their nakedness and that, suddenly, they seemed to me to be dangerous.

On the other hand, I let my hair grow long.

That is all that my brand-new being, still unoccupied, found for itself to do. I thought it would give rise to acts that would surprise me; but later on; later on, I told myself — when that being was further developed. Forced to live in a state of expectation, I maintained, like Descartes, a temporary mode of action. Thus, it was possible for Marceline not to notice anything. It's true that the different look in my eyes and, especially on the day when I showed up beardless, the new expression in my features, might perhaps have worried her, but she already loved me too much to see me clearly; moreover, I reassured her to the best of my ability. It was important that she should not disturb my self-exploration; therefore, to hide it from her observation, I had to dissimulate.

And so the man Marceline loved, the man she had married, was not my "new being." And I repeated that to myself, in order to stimulate myself to conceal it. Thus, I offered her merely an image of myself that, to the extent that it was constant and faithful to the past, became daily more false.

My relationship to Marceline, therefore, remained the same, while waiting — although heightened daily by a steadily growing love. Even my dissimulation (if that name can be given to my need to protect my thoughts from her judgment of them), my dissimulation made it grow. I mean that this mental process made me think about Marceline constantly. Perhaps that necessity to lie was rather painful to me at first; but I soon came to understand that the things considered to be most evil (lying, to mention only that) are only hard to do as long as you have never done them; but that all of them quickly become easy, pleasant and enjoyable to repeat, and soon seem natural to you. Thus, as with everything that calls for overcoming an initial distaste, I finally took pleasure in that very dissimulation, in lingering over it, equating it with the use of my unknown faculties. And every day I moved further into a richer and fuller life, toward a more delicious happiness.

VIII

The road from Ravello to Sorrento is so beautiful that, on that morning, I wished never to see anything more beautiful on earth. The warm roughness of the rocks, the expanse of sky, the fragrances, the clarity, all filled me with the delightful pleasure of living and contented me to such a degree that I seemed to be inhabited by nothing other than a weightless joy; memories or regrets, hope or desire, future and past were silent; I no longer knew anything of life except what each instant brought and took away. "O physical joy!" I shouted; "reliable rhythm of my muscles! Good health! . . ."

I had set out early in the morning, before Marceline, whose joy, too calm, would have lessened mine, just as her pace would have slowed mine. She was to rejoin me by carriage, at Positano, where we would have lunch.

I was nearing Positano when the sound of wheels, providing the bass to a weird chant, made me turn around at once. And at first I could see nothing, because of a bend in the road, which at that spot hugs the cliff; then suddenly a carriage came into sight, moving at an excessive speed; it was Marceline's. The driver was singing at the top of his voice, making broad gestures, standing up on his seat, ferociously whipping the frightened horse. What a brute! He passed in front of me, leaving me just enough time to get out of the way, not stopping when I called him. . . . I darted after them, but the carriage was going too fast. I was trembling not only at the thought of seeing Marceline suddenly fall out, but also at the thought of her remaining inside; if the horse gave a brusque start, she could be thrown into the sea. . . . All at once the horse collapsed. Marceline got out, wanted to run away; but I was already beside her. As soon as the driver saw me, he greeted me with frightful oaths. I was furious at that man; at his first insult I dashed over and brutally threw him down from his seat. I rolled on the ground with him, but I didn't lose my advantage; he seemed dazed by his fall, and soon was even more so, thanks to a punch I delivered right in his face when I saw that he intended to bite me. Yet I didn't let go of him, pressing on his chest with my knee and trying to gain control of his arms. I looked at his hideous face that my fist had just made uglier; he was spitting, drooling, bleeding, swearing — oh, what a horrible creature! Yes! It seemed justified to throttle him — and I might have done it . . . at least, I felt capable of it; and I really believe that only the idea of the police stopped me.

I finally succeeded, with great efforts, to tie up the lunatic tightly. I threw him into the carriage like a sack.

Ah! Afterwards, what looks and what kisses we exchanged! The danger hadn't been great; but I had had to show my strength, and in order to protect her. It had immediately seemed to me that I could give up my life for her . . . and give it all happily. . . . The horse had stood up again. Leaving the inside of the carriage to the drunkard, we both climbed onto his regular seat and, driving to the best of our ability, we were able to reach Positano, then Sorrento.

It was that night that I first slept with Marceline.

Have you understood, or must I tell you again, that I was like a novice in matters of love? Maybe it was to its novelty that our wedding night owed its grace. . . . For it seems to me, looking back on it today, that that first night was the only one, so much did the expectation and the surprise of love add to the sensual pleasure — so much does a single night suffice for the expression of the greatest love, and so much does my memory insist on recalling it to me uniquely. It was the laughter of a moment, in which our souls were mingled. . . . But I believe that there is a point in love, a single point, which one's soul later seeks in vain to surpass; that the effort it expends to revive its happiness wears it out; that nothing obstructs happiness as much as the memory of happiness. Unfortunately, I remember that night. . . .

Out hotel was outside town, surrounded by gardens and orchards; a very wide balcony formed an extension to our room; branches brushed against it. The dawn entered freely through our wide-open casement. I raised myself gently, and tenderly leaned over Marceline. She was sleeping; she seemed to be smiling as she slept. It seemed to me, now that I was stronger, that I perceived her as being more delicate, and that her gracefulness lay in her fragility. Chaotic thoughts swirled through my head. It occurred to me that she wasn't lying when she said I meant everything to her; then, immediately: "But what am I doing to make her happy? I neglect her almost all day long every day; she expects everything from me, and I desert her! . . . Oh, poor, poor Marceline!" Tears filled my eyes. In vain I sought a kind of excuse in my past physical weakness; what need did I now have of constant attentions and selfishness? Wasn't I now stronger than she? . . .

The smile had left her cheeks; the dawn, although gilding everything, caused me to see her suddenly sad and pale — and perhaps the approach of morning was inclining me toward anguish: "Will *I*, in my turn, have to take care of *you* some day, worry about *you*, Marceline?" I shouted inside myself. I shuddered; and, completely chilled with love, pity and affection, I gently planted the most tender, loving and pious of kisses between her two closed eyes.

IX

The few days we spent at Sorrento were smiling, very calm days. Had I ever enjoyed such repose, such happiness? Would I enjoy the like in the future? . . . I was constantly in Marceline's vicinity; less occupied with myself, I occupied myself more with her, and found in chatting with her the pleasure I had taken on the previous days in being silent.

It was still a surprise to me at first that our wandering life, with which I was sure I was completely contented, appealed to her merely as a temporary state of affairs; but immediately the idleness of that life came across to me; I accepted the fact that it was not to last, and for the first time — as a desire to work sprang up anew out of the very feeling of uselessness which my restored health now generated — I spoke seriously about going back; from the joy Marceline showed at my remark, I realized she had been thinking about it for some time.

Nevertheless, the various historical studies I was starting to think about again no longer held the same appeal for me. As I told you: since my illness, the abstract, neutral knowledge of the past seemed futile to me, and if, earlier, I had been able to busy myself with philological research — for example, striving to isolate the part played by Gothic influence in the deformation of the Latin language, but ignoring and failing to appreciate the figures of Theodoric, Cassiodorus and Amalaswintha* and their wonderful passions, while finding excitement merely in the written records and in the relics of their life — now those very records, and all of philology, were no more to me than a means of penetrating more deeply into those existences whose savage grandeur and nobility were clear to me. I resolved to occupy myself further with that era, to

---

* Major figures of the early sixth century, a crucial turning point between classical antiquity and the medieval period. Theodoric was ruler of the Ostrogothic kingdom in Italy; his daughter Amalaswintha acted as regent for her young son Athalaric; Cassiodorus was a Roman adviser to the court.

confine myself for a time to the final years of the empire of the Goths, and to take advantage of our forthcoming trip to Ravenna, the theater of its demise.

But — shall I admit it? — it was the figure of the young king Athalaric that most attracted me to the subject. I pictured this child of fifteen, secretly incited by the Goths, rebelling against his mother Amalaswintha, balking at his Latin upbringing, throwing off civilization as a stallion throws off a cumbersome harness, and, preferring the society of uncultured Goths to that of the overly proper and aged Cassiodorus, enjoying for a few years, along with rough favorites of his own age, a violent, sensual and unbridled life, only to die at eighteen, thoroughly wasted and sodden with debauchery. I found in that tragic yearning for a more savage and pristine condition some part of what Marceline smilingly called "my crisis." I was seeking some permission to bend at least my mind to it, since I was no longer employing my body in it; and in the terrible death of Athalaric I convinced myself as best I could that a lesson was to be learned.

Before Ravenna, where we would thus linger for two weeks, we would rapidly see Rome and Florence, then, leaving aside Venice and Verona, we would hasten the end of our journey and make no more stops before Paris. I found a brand-new pleasure in discussing our future with Marceline; a certain indecision still remained concerning the way we would spend the summer; both of us were tired of traveling and didn't wish to set out on another trip; I hoped for as much peace and quiet as possible for my studies; and we thought about an income-producing property between Lisieux and Pont-l'Évêque, in the greenest part of Normandy — a property once owned by my mother, where I had spent a few summers of my childhood with her but which I hadn't returned to since her death. My father had entrusted its maintenance and stewardship to a bailiff, elderly by now, who used to collect the tenant farmers' rent for him and now sent it regularly to us. A large, very pleasant house, in a garden traversed by running streams, had left me with delightful memories; it was called La Morinière; I thought it would be pleasant to live there.

For the following winter I spoke about visiting Rome — to work, no longer as a tourist this time. . . . But that last plan was quickly upset: among the large accumulation of mail that had long awaited us at Naples, a letter suddenly informed us that, a chair having become vacant at the Collège de France,* my name had been proposed several

---

* A particularly distinguished college in Paris.

times; it was only a temporary position, but of just such a type as would allow me greater freedom in the future; the friend who informed me of all this indicated a few simple steps I should take if I was willing to accept — and urged me strongly to accept. I hesitated, especially since at first I regarded it as a kind of slavery; then it occurred to me that it might be interesting to expound my researches on Cassiodorus in a lecture course. . . . The pleasure I would thereby give Marceline was what finally decided me. And once my mind was made up, I saw only the advantages in it.

In the scholarly world of Rome and Florence my father had maintained several contacts, people with whom I myself had corresponded. They gave me all the means to pursue any research I wished, at Ravenna and elsewhere; I was now thinking of nothing but work. Marceline contrived to foster it with a thousand charming attentions and a thousand kindnesses.

Our happiness during this final stage of our journey was so unruffled, so calm, that I can no longer recount any of it. The most beautiful works of men are implacably sorrowful. What would a narrative of happiness be like? All that can be described is what prepares it, and then what destroys it. And now I have told you everything that had prepared it.

PART TWO

I

WE ARRIVED at La Morinière in the first days of July, having stopped in Paris only just long enough to shop for necessities and pay a very few visits.

La Morinière, as I said, is located between Lisieux and Pont-l'Évêque, in the shadiest, dampest region I know of. Several foothill valleys, narrow and gently curving, come to an end, not far distant, in the very wide Auge valley, which suddenly flattens out all the way to the sea. No horizon; brushwoods full of mystery; only a few fields, but meadows everywhere, pastures with gentle slopes, the thick grass of which is mown twice a year, where numerous apple trees unite their shade when the sun is low, where flocks graze freely; in every hollow, water: pond, pool or stream; continual babbling is heard.

Ah! How well I recognized the house! — its blue roofs, its walls of brick and stone, its moats, the reflections in the still waters. . . . It was an old house with room enough for more than a dozen people; with the help of Marceline, three servants and sometimes myself, we had our hands full to recall even a part of it to life. Our old bailiff, who was named Bocage, had already had a few rooms prepared to the best of his ability; the old furniture reawakened from its twenty years' slumber; everything had remained just as I saw it in my memory, the wainscoting not too dilapidated, the rooms easily made livable. To welcome us more heartily, Bocage had filled with flowers every vase he could find. He had had the main courtyard and the closest park walks hoed and raked. When we arrived, the house was lit by the last sunbeam, and from the valley in front of it a stationary mist had risen which partly veiled, partly revealed the stream. Even before arriving, I suddenly recognized the smell of the grass; and when I once more heard the high-pitched calls of the swallows circling around the house, the entire past rose up as if it had been awaiting me and, now recognizing me, wished to envelop me again as I approached.

After a few days the house became nearly comfortable; I could have set to work; I delayed, still listening to my past being recalled to me in great detail, and then soon preoccupied by an emotion that was all too novel: a week after our arrival, Marceline told me in confidence that she was pregnant.

I thought that from then on I owed her additional attention, that she had a right to more affection; thus, at least for some time after learning her secret, I spent nearly every moment of the day near her. We would go and sit near the forest, on the bench where I once used to sit with my mother; there, every instant became more deeply pleasurable to us, time passed by more unnoticed. If no clear memory stands out from that period of my life, it is not because my gratitude toward it is less keen — but surely because all things blended into it, mingling together in a uniform feeling of well-being, in which evening followed morning with no abrupt jolts, in which the days were linked one to another without surprises.

Slowly I resumed my work, my mind calm, fresh, sure of its powers, facing the future with confidence and without fever, my willpower seemingly tamed and seemingly ready to take the advice of these temperate surroundings.

"Without doubt," I thought, "the example of this land where everything develops toward fruition, toward a beneficent harvest, is sure to have the most desirable influence on me." I admired the calm future promised by those sturdy oxen, those cows big with calf, in those opulent meadows. The apple trees, planted in orderly rows on the appropriate hillsides, announced wonderful crops that summer; I dreamed about the rich load of fruit beneath which their boughs would soon be bending. From that orderly abundance, from that enjoyable subservience, from those radiant plantings, a harmony took form, no longer accidental but planned, a rhythm and beauty that were both human and natural, in which no one could tell what to admire most, since the fecund eruption of untrammeled nature and the knowledgeable efforts of man to regulate it were blended in such perfect agreement. "What would those efforts matter," I thought, "without the powerful savagery that they control? What would become of the wild drive of that overflowing sap without the intelligent effort that channels it and leads it laughingly toward profusion?" And I abandoned myself to dreams of lands in which all forces were so well regulated, all expenses so fully recouped, all exchanges so fair, that the slightest falling off would become noticeable;

then, applying my dream to real life, I constructed an ethical code that became a science of the fullest utilization of one's self through intelligent restraint.

At that time, into what depths of my mind were my stormy ideas of past days sinking? Where were they hiding? I was so calm that it seemed they had never existed. The waves of my love had covered them up completely. . . .

Meanwhile old Bocage was flaunting his zeal to us; he was managing, overseeing, giving advice; his need to find himself indispensable was painfully evident. In order not to hurt his feelings, we had to examine his accounts and listen to every detail of his endless explanations. Even that didn't satisfy him; I had to accompany him over the grounds. His sententious saws, his continual speeches, his obvious self-satisfaction, his display of honesty, irritated me before very long; he was becoming more and more pressing, and I would have approved of any means to regain my comfort — when an unexpected event gave my relationship to him a different character: one evening, Bocage announced to me that he was expecting his son Charles the next day.

I said "Oh!," hardly caring, since up to that time I hadn't concerned myself much with any children Bocage might have; then, seeing that my indifference upset him, that he was expecting some sign of interest and surprise from me, I asked where he was at the moment.

"On a model farm near Alençon," Bocage replied.

"By now he must be about . . . ," I continued, calculating the age of this son of whose existence I hadn't known before then, and speaking slowly enough to give him time to interrupt me. . . .

"Over seventeen," Bocage resumed. "He wasn't much more than four when your mother died. Oh, he's a big fellow now; soon he'll know more than his father. . . ." And once Bocage got going, nothing could stop him any more, no matter how much I manifested my weariness.

The next day the matter had slipped my mind when, near the end of the day, Charles, having just arrived, came to pay his respects to Marceline and me. He was a good-looking dog, so bursting with health, so supple, so well built, that even the horrible city clothes he had put on in our honor failed to make him too ridiculous; his shy blushes hardly added to the fine natural ruddiness of his complexion. He looked as if he were only fifteen, because the brightness of his eyes had remained so childlike; he expressed himself very lucidly, without painful timidity, and, unlike his father, didn't talk just for the sake of it. I don't remember what remarks we exchanged that first evening; busy observing him, I found nothing to say to him and let Marceline speak to him. But the

next day, for the first time, without waiting for old Bocage to fetch me I
went out to the farm, where I knew some construction had begun.

It concerned repairs to a pool. This pool, the size of a large pond, was
leaking; the source of the leak was known and the task was to cement it.
To do that it was first necessary to empty the pool, which hadn't been
done for fifteen years. It contained a large number of carp and tench,
some very big, which no longer swam higher than the bottom. I was
eager to raise some of them in the waters of the moats and give some
to the workers, so that for this once an enjoyable fishing expedition was
combined with the labor, as was evident from the unusual excitement
aroused on the farm; some children from the neighborhood had come
and were mingling with the workers. Marceline herself was to join us a
little later.

The water level had already been dropping for some time when I
got there. At times a massive shudder suddenly rippled the surface,
revealing the brown backs of the nervous fish. In the puddles at the
edge, splashing children were catching shiny small fry, which they
threw into pails full of clear water. The water of the pool, which was
further troubled by the agitation of the fish, was dull-colored and was
getting more opaque every minute. The number of fish exceeded all expectations; four farmhands were drawing some out by dipping in their
hands randomly. I was sorry that Marceline wasn't there yet and I was
just about to run and get her when a few shouts announced the first
eels. No one managed to catch any; they were slipping through people's
fingers. Charles, who up to then had remained near his father on the
bank, could no longer restrain himself; he suddenly took off his shoes
and socks, laid down his jacket and vest, then, tucking up his trousers
and shirt sleeves very high, he resolutely walked into the ooze. At once
I imitated him.

"Well, Charles," I shouted, "is it a good thing that you got back
yesterday?"

He made no reply, but looked at me, all smiles, already completely
occupied with his fishing. I soon called him over to help me close in on
a big eel; we joined hands in order to seize it. . . . Then, after that one,
there was another; the mud was splashing us in the face; at times we
suddenly sank in and the water rose to our thighs, we were soon soaking
wet. In the ardor of the game we hardly exchanged a few shouted words,
a few sentences; but, at the end of the day, I noticed that I was calling Charles *tu*,* without remembering clearly when I had begun. This

---

* The familiar form of "you," as opposed to the formal *vous*.

shared activity had taught us more about each other than a long conversation could have done. Marceline hadn't come yet and didn't come, but by now I no longer regretted her absence; it seemed to me that she might have troubled our enjoyment a little.

On the very next day, I went out to find Charles on the farm. The two of us headed toward the woods.

Since I was little acquainted with my property and didn't fret much at that lack of acquaintance, I was greatly surprised to see that Charles was very well acquainted with it, and with the boundaries of the tenant farms; he informed me of a fact I was hardly aware of, that I had six tenants, that I might have been able to receive sixteen to eighteen thousand francs in rent and, if I was now receiving just barely half of that, it was because the money was being lost in all kinds of repairs and payments to middlemen. The way he smiled now and then when inspecting the planted fields soon made me doubt whether the use being made of my land was as excellent as I had at first believed and as Bocage gave me to understand; I questioned Charles on that subject, and that totally practical kind of intelligence which irritated me in Bocage managed to amuse me in that youngster. Day after day we resumed our walks; the estate was vast and, after we had searched out all its nooks and crannies, we started over again more methodically. Charles didn't hide from me his annoyance at the sight of certain badly tended fields, areas overrun by furze, thistles and rank grasses; he made me share in his hatred for fallow ground and his hopes for better-supervised plantings.

"But," I would say to him at first, "who suffers from this mediocre maintenance? Merely the tenant farmer, right? If the income from his farm varies, that doesn't make his rent vary."

And Charles would get a little annoyed. "You don't understand at all," he had the boldness to reply, and I would immediately smile. "You're considering only the income and forgetting that the capital investment depreciates. When your land is improperly cultivated, its value slowly goes down."

"If, under better cultivation, it could bring in more, I don't see why the tenants shouldn't apply themselves; I know they're too self-seeking not to harvest as much as they can."

Charles continued, "You aren't taking into account the increase in the work force. These plots of land are sometimes far from the main farms. If they were planted they'd bring in nothing or next to nothing, but at least they wouldn't go to ruin. . . ."

And the conversation would continue. Sometimes, as we strode across the fields, we would seem to be going over the same topics for an hour at a time; but I was listening and gradually becoming instructed.

"After all, this is a matter for your father," I said to him one day, losing my patience. Charles blushed a little, and said: "My father is old; he already has his hands full drawing up the leases and seeing that the buildings are kept up and the rents are properly collected. His goal here is not one of reform."

"What reforms would *you* suggest?" I went on. But then he would hold back, claiming not to have a sufficient grasp of the matter; it was only by insisting that I compelled him to explain himself.

"To take away from the tenants all plots of land that they leave unplanted," was his advice at last. "If the farmers let a part of their fields lie fallow, that proves that they have more than enough to pay you out of; or, if they want to hold onto all they have, raise their rent. They're all lazy in this part of the country," he added.

Of the six farms it seemed I owned, the one I most enjoyed visiting was located on the hill that overlooked La Morinière; it was called La Valterie; the farmer who leased it was not unpleasant; I liked chatting with him. Closer to La Morinière, a farm known as "the manor house farm" was rented on a partial sharecropping arrangement that, in the absence of the landlord, allowed Bocage to possess part of the livestock. Now that my mistrust had been aroused, I started to suspect honest Bocage himself, if not of swindling me, at least of allowing me to be swindled by a number of people. True, one stable and one cowshed were set apart for me, but it was soon clear to me that they had been invented solely to permit the tenant to feed his cows and horses on my oats and hay. Up to then I had lent a kindly ear to even the most unlikely reports that Bocage occasionally gave me on the subject: deaths, malformations and diseases of the cattle — I accepted it all. I had not yet thought it possible that, whenever one of the tenant's cows got sick, no more was needed to make it one of my cows; nor that, if one of my cows was feeling fine, no more was needed to make it the tenant's; nevertheless, some remarks Charles let drop carelessly and a few observations of my own began to enlighten me; then my mind, once awakened, started racing.

Alerted by me, Marceline went over all the accounts minutely, but couldn't put her finger on any error; Bocage's honesty found a safe berth there. What should I do? Let things take their course. But at least, secretly annoyed, I now examined the animals, though without being too conspicuous about it.

I had four horses and ten cows; they were enough to torment me. Of my four horses, there was one still called "the colt" even though he was over three; he was being trained at the moment; I was starting to take an interest in this when, one fine day, they came and announced to me that he was completely unmanageable, that nothing could ever be done with him and that it was best for me to get rid of him. As if I might wish to doubt it, they had caused him to break the front of a small cart, bloodying his hocks on it.

That day it was hard for me to keep calm, and what restrained me was Bocage's embarrassment. After all, there was more weakness than malevolence in him, I thought; his hirelings were to blame; but they received no sense of being supervised.

I went out into the courtyard to see the colt. As soon as he heard me approach, a farmhand who was beating him started to pat him; I acted as if I hadn't seen a thing. I didn't know a great deal about horses, but that colt looked fine to me; he was a half-bred light bay with a remarkably svelte build; his eyes were extremely alert, and both his mane and tail were nearly flaxen yellow. I made sure he wasn't injured, ordered his scratches to be dressed and left again without another word.

In the evening, as soon as I saw Charles, I tried to elicit his opinion of the colt.

"I think he's very gentle," he said, "but they don't know how to handle him; they'll drive him crazy on you."

"How would *you* handle him?"

"Would you entrust him to me for a week, sir? I'll be responsible."

"And what will you do for him?"

"You'll see. . . ."

The next day Charles took the colt out to a corner of the meadow shaded by a magnificent walnut tree and bordered by the stream; I went there, accompanied by Marceline. It is one of my most vivid memories. With a rope a few yards long Charles had tied the colt to a stake firmly planted in the ground. It seems that the colt, excessively nervous, had resisted furiously for a while; now, cooled down, tired out, he was moving in a circle in a calmer manner; his trot, surprisingly springy, was a pleasure to watch, as bewitching as a dance. Charles, at the center of the circle, avoiding the rope at each revolution by a sudden jump, was inciting him or calming him down with words; he was holding a big whip in his hand, but I didn't see him use it. Everything in his manner and gestures, because of his youth and happiness, lent that task the beautiful fervency of pleasure. Suddenly, I don't know how, he bestrode the animal; it had slowed its gait, then had stopped; he had patted it a while, then suddenly I saw him mounted, self-confident, keeping his seat by barely grasping the mane, laughing, leaning over and continuing his caress. The colt had barely jibbed for an instant; now he was resuming his uniform trot, so beautiful, so supple, that I envied Charles and told him so.

"A few more days of training and the saddle won't tickle him any more; in two weeks, ma'am, you should have no fear to ride him yourself: he'll be gentle as a ewe-lamb."

He was speaking the truth; a few days later, the horse allowed himself to be patted, saddled and led around without mistrust; and Marceline could have mounted him if her condition had permitted her that exercise.

"You ought to try him, sir," Charles said to me.

That is something I would never have done alone; but Charles suggested saddling another farm horse for himself; the pleasure of accompanying him decided me.

How grateful I was to my mother for having taken me to riding school when I was very young! The distant memory of those first lessons now came in handy. I didn't feel too surprised at sitting in a saddle; after a few moments all fear was gone and I felt at ease. The horse Charles was riding was heavy, of no particular breed, but not at all unpleasant to look at; above all, Charles sat him well. We acquired the habit of riding out a little every day; we preferred to set out very early, while the grass was bright with dew; we would reach the edge of the woods; dripping-wet hazel trees that we shook as we went by would soak us; suddenly the horizon would open up; it was the vast Auge valley; in the distance you could imagine the sea. We would pause a moment without alighting; the rising sun tinged, broke up and dispersed the mists; then we would resume at a fast trot; we would spend time on the farm; work was just beginning; we would savor that proud pleasure of being out before the laborers were and then towering over them; after that, we would leave them all at once; I would get back to La Morinière just as Marceline was waking up.

I would return drunk with the fresh air, dazed with the speed of my ride, my limbs a little stiff with a sensually enjoyable weariness, my mind full of health, appetite and vigor. Marceline approved of and encouraged my fancies. Coming home, still wearing my gaiters, I would bring to the bed, where she lingered awaiting me, that fragrance of moist leaves which she told me she liked. And she would listen to my account of our ride, the awakening of the fields, the resumption of work. . . . She seemed to derive as much pleasure from feeling the life in me as from living herself. And so I soon took unfair advantage of that pleasure; our outings grew longer, and sometimes I wouldn't get back to the house until about noon.

And yet, as much as I could, I reserved the latter part of the day and the evening for the preparation of my course. My work was progressing; I was satisfied with it and I didn't consider it impossible that, later on, it might be worthwhile to gather my lectures together into a book. By a sort of natural reaction, while my life was becoming organized and regulated, and I took pleasure in regulating and organizing everything around me, I was more and more captivated by the primitive ethics of the Goths, and at the same time that, throughout my course, I strove to praise and justify their lack of culture — with a boldness for which I was sharply criticized afterwards — I was laboriously contriving to control, if not to eliminate, everything that might recall that lack of culture both in my surroundings and in myself. To what an extent I carried that wisdom or, rather, that folly!

Two of my tenants, whose leases were to expire at Christmas, were eager to renew them and came to see me; they intended to sign the customary paper known as an "undertaking to lease." Trusting in Charles's assurances and aroused by his daily conversations, I awaited the tenants with determination. They, secure in the knowledge that a tenant is hard to replace, at first demanded a reduction in the rent. Their amazement was all the greater when I read them the "undertakings" I had composed myself, in which I not only refused to lower the tenancy charges, but also took away from them certain plots of land that I had observed they weren't using. At first they pretended to laugh it off: I was joking. What did those pieces of land matter to me? They were worthless; and if the farmers did nothing with them, it was because nothing *could* be done. . . . Then, seeing I was serious, they got stubborn; I, on my side, was stubborn, too. They thought they could frighten me by threatening to leave. I had been waiting for just those words.

"Ha! Well, leave if you want! I'm not holding you," I said to them. I took the "undertakings to lease" and tore them up right before their eyes.

Thus I was left with over two hundred fifty acres on my hands. For some time now I had been planning to entrust the chief stewardship of that land to Bocage, with the clear intention of thereby giving it to Charles indirectly; besides, I really wasn't thinking seriously: the very risk of the undertaking tempted me. The tenants weren't going to move out until Christmas; by then we could still set things right. I informed Charles; I was at once displeased by his joy; he couldn't hide it; it made me even more aware that he was much too young. The time was now pressing; we were at that part of the year when the first harvests leave the fields free for the first plowing. By an established convention, there is no gap between the work done by the outgoing tenant and that done by the new one, the outgoing man abandoning his property parcel by parcel as soon as the crops are in. I feared, as a kind of revenge, the animosity of the two tenants I had let go; on the contrary, it suited them to pretend to be perfectly accommodating toward me (I learned only later the benefit they derived thereby). I took advantage of that by spending time, morning and evening, on their land, which was soon to revert to me. Autumn was beginning; I had to hire more men to speed up the plowing and sowing; we had bought harrows, clod crushers, plows; I rode around observing, directing the work, finding pleasure in giving orders myself, in being the master.

Meanwhile, in the neighboring meadows the tenants were harvesting the apples; they were falling, rolling in the thick grass, more plentiful than in any other year; the workers were all too few for the task; others came from neighboring villages; they were hired for a week; Charles and I sometimes amused ourselves by helping them. Some were prodding the branches with long poles to make the late fruit fall; a separate harvest was made of the fruit that had dropped by itself, too ripe, often bruised, crushed among the high grass; it was impossible to walk without stepping on some. The smell arising from the meadow, acrid and over-sweet, mingled with that of the plowed fields.

The autumn was advancing. The mornings of the last fine days are the coolest and clearest. Sometimes the moist atmosphere turned the distant prospect blue, made it seem even farther away, turned an outing into a journey; the countryside seemed magnified; sometimes, on the other hand, the abnormal transparency of the air brought the horizon up close; it seemed it could be reached in one wingbeat; and I'm not sure which of these two phenomena generated more languor. My personal work was nearly finished; at least I said so, in order to distract myself from it more rashly. The time I was no longer spending on the farm I devoted to Marceline. We went out into the garden together; we walked slowly, she languidly and weighing on my arm; we went and sat on a bench from which we overlooked the little valley that the evening was filling with light. She had an affectionate way of resting on my shoulder; and we would remain that way until evening, feeling the day melting away inside us, making no gesture, speaking no word. . . . Our love was already capable of enveloping itself in that much silence! That's because Marceline's love was already stronger than any words she could find to express it, and because at times I was nearly tortured by that love. Just as a breeze sometimes ripples a very placid body of water, her slightest emotion was visible on her brow; she was listening to a new life mysteriously stirring within her; I would bend over her as if over deep, pure waters in which, as far as the eye could reach, nothing but love could be seen. Oh, if that still was happiness, I know I wanted to hold onto it from then on, the way you want to hold onto running water in your cupped hands, though in vain; yet I already felt, alongside happiness, something other than happiness, which was certainly coloring my love, but with autumnal colors.

The autumn was advancing. The grass, wetter every morning, no longer dried at all inside the edge of the woods; at the break of dawn it was white. The ducks on the waters of the moats flapped their wings; they made wild movements; at times they could be seen ascending and making full circles around La Morinière, calling loudly, flying noisily. One morning we no longer saw them; Bocage had shut them in. Charles told me they are shut in that way every autumn, at migration time. And, a few days later, the weather changed. One evening, suddenly, there was a big gust, a breath from the sea, strong, with undivided force, bringing the north wind and the rain, carrying off the migratory birds. Marceline's condition, the chores attendant on moving into a new place, the first concerns about my course, would have been enough to call us back to the city. The harsh season, which was beginning early, drove us out.

True, the farm work was to take me back in November. I had been quite vexed at learning Bocage's arrangements for the winter; he announced to me his wish to send Charles back to the model farm, where, he claimed, he still had quite a lot to learn; I chatted with him for some time, using all the arguments I could muster, but I couldn't make him back down; the most he would agree to was to curtail those studies somewhat so that Charles could return a little earlier. Bocage didn't conceal from me the fact that the cultivation of the two farms couldn't be managed without great difficulty; but, he informed me, he had in mind two reliable farmers whom he expected to sign up; they would be a combination of rent-payers, sharecroppers and hired hands; the arrangement was too novel for that region for him to hope for much good from it; but, he said, it was I who had wanted it that way. That conversation took place toward the end of October. In the first days of November, we moved into our new apartment in Paris.

II

We moved into S. Street, near Passy.* The apartment, which had been suggested to us by a brother of Marceline, and which we had been able to visit the last time we were in Paris, was much larger than the one my father had left me, and Marceline had cause for some concern, not only over the higher rent, but also over all the expenses we were going to let ourselves in for. I countered all her fears with an insincere objection to makeshift arrangements; I even forced myself to believe it and purposely exaggerated it. Certainly the various costs of setting up our home there would go beyond our means that year, but our fortune, already sizable, was bound to increase; for that I counted on my lecture course, the publication of my book and even (what folly!) on the new income from my farms. Thus I didn't blink at any expense; at each new outlay I told myself that I was strengthening my family ties all the more, and I believed that, at the same time, I was also rooting out any wanderlust I might feel, or might fear I would feel, in myself.

In the first days, from morning till evening, our time was spent on errands; and, even though Marceline's brother very obligingly offered his services to spare us several of them, before long Marceline felt very tired. Then, instead of the rest she needed, as soon as we were set up she had to receive one caller after another; the distance at which we had lived up till then made them flock to us now, and Marceline, no longer accustomed to social ways, was unable either to curtail the length of the visits or to say she wasn't in; in the evening I would find her exhausted; and, if I wasn't worried about her weariness, knowing its natural cause, at least I strove to lessen it, often by receiving our guests in her stead, which I hardly enjoyed, and sometimes by repaying the visits, which I enjoyed even less.

I've never been a brilliant conversationalist; the frivolity of salons, their wit, is something I could take no pleasure in; nevertheless I *had* frequented some in the past — but how far away that time was! What had happened since? In the company of others I felt dull, sad, troublesome, both ill at ease and causing others to be the same. . . . Through a remarkable piece of bad luck, you, whom I already considered as my only true friends, weren't in Paris and weren't expected back for some time. Would I have had less difficulty in talking to you? Would you per-

---

* A fashionable upper middle-class neighborhood in Paris.

haps have understood me better than I did myself? But of all that was developing inside me, and which I'm telling you today, what did I know? The future seemed all planned out to me, and I had never felt in firmer control of it.

And even if I had been more aware, what aid against myself could I find in Hubert, Didier, Maurice and so many others whom you know and of whom you have the same opinion as mine? Unfortunately, I very soon realized the impossibility of making them understand me. From the very first chats we had, I saw that, in a way, I was compelled by them to play a false part, to resemble the man they believed I still was, or else appear to be pretending; and, to make life easier, therefore, I did pretend to share the thoughts and tastes that people ascribed to me. You can't be sincere and seem to be sincere at one and the same time.

It was with somewhat more enjoyment that I renewed acquaintance with the people in my field, archaeologists and philologists, but in chatting with them I found hardly more pleasure and no more emotion than in leafing through good historical dictionaries. At first I hoped to find a somewhat more direct understanding of life in some novelists and some poets; but, if they possessed that understanding, I must confess they hardly showed it; it seemed to me as if most of them weren't living at all, but were contented with seeming to live, and almost considered life as an annoying obstacle to writing. And I couldn't blame them for it; and I won't affirm that the mistake wasn't on my side. . . . Anyway, what did I mean by "living"? That is exactly what I would have liked someone to tell me. This group and that spoke deftly, about the various happenings of life, never about what motivates those happenings.

As for the few philosophers, whose role it would have been to instruct me, I had known for some time what I could expect from them; whether mathematicians or Neo-Kantians, they kept as far away as possible from reality, which might disturb them, and were no more concerned with it than the algebraist is with the real existence of the quantities that he measures.

Back home with Marceline, I didn't conceal from her the tedium which that socializing caused me.

"They're all alike," I told her. "Each one of them is interchangeable. When I speak to one of them, I think I'm talking to the whole group."

"But, dear," Marceline would reply, "you can't expect each of them to be different from all the rest."

"The more they resemble one another, the more they differ from me."

And then I would resume more sadly: "None of them has had the capacity to be sick. They live, they give the appearance of living and of not knowing they're alive. Moreover, since I've been keeping company with them, I'm no longer living, either. To take just one day, what did I accomplish today? I had to leave you by nine; before going I just barely had the time to read a little; that was the only good moment in the day. Your brother was waiting for me at the real-estate agent's, and after the agent he didn't let me alone; I had to see the upholsterer with him; he bothered me at the cabinetmaker's and I was only able to ditch him at Gaston's; I lunched in the neighborhood with Philippe, then I looked up Louis, who was waiting for me at the café; with him I listened to Théodore's absurd lecture, complimenting him on it as we left; in order to decline his invitation for Sunday, I had to accompany him to Arthur's; with Arthur I went to see a watercolor exhibition; I went to leave my card at Albertine's and Julie's. . . . Worn out, I come home and find you as exhausted as I am, after seeing Adeline, Marthe, Jeanne, Sophie . . . and now, in the evening, when I review all these occupations of the day, I feel my day was so pointless and it seems so empty to me that I'd like to catch it again as it flies away and recommence it hour by hour, and I'm so sad I could cry."

And yet I couldn't have said what I meant by "living," or if the taste I had acquired for a more spacious and well-ventilated life, one less constrained and less concerned about others, wasn't the simple secret of my irritation. That secret seemed much more mysterious to me: a secret like a resurrected man's, I thought; for I remained a stranger amid the others, like someone returning from the dead. And at first I merely experienced a rather painful confusion; but soon a very novel feeling manifested itself. I assure you, I hadn't been at all proud at the time those works were published which garnered me so much praise. Was it pride now? Perhaps; but at least not a hint of vanity was mixed with it. For the first time, it was the consciousness of my own worth; that which set me apart, which distinguished me from the others, was what really counted; that which no one but me was saying or could say, was what I had to say.

My course began soon afterward; since the subject carried me away, I poured all my new-found passion into my first lecture. Referring to the final stage of Latin civilization, I depicted artistic culture as an emanation from a given people, like a secretion that at first is diagnostic of a plethora, a superabundance of health, then immediately congeals and hardens, cutting off all direct contact between the mind and nature, hiding the diminution of life beneath the persistent semblance of life, an unyielding sheath in which the confined spirit languishes and soon withers, then dies. Finally, carrying my train of thought to the extreme, I stated that culture, which is born of life, becomes the killer of life.

Historians found fault with what they called a tendency toward overhasty generalizations. Others found fault with my method; and those who complimented me were those who had understood me least.

It was on leaving after my lecture that I ran across Menalcas* again for the first time. I had never associated with him much, and shortly before my marriage he had set out again on one of those distant explorations which sometimes used to deprive us of his company for over a year. In the past I didn't like him much; he seemed haughty and wasn't interested in the life I led. And so I was surprised to see him at my first lecture. I liked even his insolence, which at first had repelled me, and the smile he gave me seemed all the more delightful to me because I knew how rare it was. Shortly before, a ridiculous, shameful, scandalous trial had given the press a handy opportunity to besmirch him; those who had been wounded by his disdain and superiority seized upon this pretext for their vengeance; and what irritated them the most was that he didn't seem to be affected by it.

He would reply to the insults, "One must let the others be right, since that consoles them for not being anything else."

But "good society" was indignant and those who, as the saying goes, "have self-respect" thought it their duty to turn away from him and thus repay him for his contempt. That was an added reason for me: attracted to him by a secret influence, I went over and embraced him cordially in front of everybody.

Seeing with whom I was chatting, the last nuisances withdrew; I remained alone with Menalcas.

After the irritating criticisms and the inept compliments, his few words on the subject of my lecture relaxed me.

"You're burning what you once worshipped," he said. "That's good. You took your time getting there; but that makes the flame all the stronger. I don't know yet whether I understand you fully; you intrigue me. I don't like to chat, but I'd like to chat with you. So please have dinner with me this evening."

"My dear Menalcas," I replied, "you seem to forget that I'm married."

"Yes, that's true," he continued; "on seeing the cordial frankness with

---

* At this period of his career, Gide, a passionate admirer of the classics, gave Greco-Roman pseudonyms to a number of his friends and to characters in his books. Menalcas is a shepherd mentioned in several of Vergil's *Eclogues*. The ancient form of the name is used here in preference to the French form, Ménalque, of the original text, just as, for example, "Theocritus" was used earlier in preference to "Théocrite."

which you had the courage to greet me, I thought you enjoyed more freedom."

I was afraid I had hurt him, and even more afraid of seeming weak; I told him I would join him after dinner.

In Paris, always a mere transient, Menalcas would stop at a hotel. For this stay he had had several rooms arranged like an apartment; he had his servants there, ate by himself, lived by himself, and he had spread out on the walls and furniture, whose banal ugliness offended him, some valuable fabrics he had brought back from Nepal and which he said he was now finally discoloring before offering them to a museum. My haste to join him had been so great that I caught him still at table when I came in; and, when I apologized for disturbing his meal, he said:

"But I have no intention of interrupting it and I expect you to let me finish it. If you had come for dinner, I would have poured you some Shiraz, that wine whose praises were sung by Hafiz,* but it's too late now; one must drink it on an empty stomach; will you have a liqueur, at least?"

I accepted, thinking he would take one, too; but, seeing that only one glass was brought, I expressed surprise.

"Excuse me," he said, "but I almost never drink any."

"Are you possibly afraid of getting tipsy?"

"Oh!" he answered, "just the opposite! But I consider sobriety to be a more powerful state of intoxication; I retain my lucidity that way."

"And you pour out drinks for others . . ."

He smiled.

"I can't expect everyone to share my virtues," he said. "It's already an accomplishment when I rediscover my vices in them. . . ."

"Do you smoke, at least?"

"Not that, either. That's an impersonal, negative intoxication, too easily obtained; in intoxication I look for a heightening, not a lessening, of life. But let's drop that. Do you know where I've just come from? From Biskra. Knowing you had just been there, I wanted to retrace your steps. What in the world had he come to Biskra for, that pedantic blind man, that bookworm? Habitually my discretion extends only to what I've been told in confidence; for what I find out by myself, I admit it, my curiosity is boundless. And so I looked around, investigated and questioned people everywhere I could. My indiscretion was of use to me, because it gave me the desire to see you again; because, in place of the plodding

---

* Great Persian poet, 14th century.

scholar I formerly saw in you, I know that now I must see . . . it's up to you to tell me what."

I felt myself blushing.

"What, then, did you find out about me, Menalcas?"

"You want to know? But don't be afraid! You're well enough acquainted with your friends and mine to know that I can't speak about you to anyone. You yourself have seen how well people understood your lecture!"

"But," I said with some slight impatience, "there's nothing to show me that I can talk to you any more than to the rest. Come on! What did you find out about me?"

"First, that you had been ill."

"But that's not at all . . ."

"Oh! that's a very significant beginning. Then, I was told that you liked going out alone, without a book (and that's when I began to be surprised), or else, when you weren't alone, you preferred the company of children to that of your wife. . . . Don't blush, or I won't tell you the rest."

"Tell it without looking at me."

"One of the children — his name was Moktir if I remember correctly — handsomer than most, more thievish and deceitful than any, seemed to me to have a lot to say on the subject; I sought out his secrets and paid for them, which, as you know, isn't easy, because I think he was still lying when he said he was no longer lying. . . . And so, tell me if what he said about you is true."

Meanwhile Menalcas had stood up and had taken from a drawer a little box, which he opened.

"Were these scissors yours?" he asked me, handing me some shapeless, rusted, blunt, buckled object; even so, it wasn't hard for me to recognize it as the little scissors Moktir had filched.

"Yes, they're the ones, they were my wife's."

"He claims to have taken them from you while you had your head turned, one day when you were alone with him in a room; but that's not the interesting part; he claims that at the moment he was hiding them in his burnoose, he realized you were observing him in a mirror and he caught sight of your reflection as you were watching him. You had seen the theft and you said nothing about it! Moktir appeared to be very surprised at that silence . . . so was I."

"I'm just as surprised at what you're telling me. What! So he knew I had caught him!"

"That's not what's important; you two were playing the game of who's cleverer; those children will always beat us at that game. You thought you had him, and it was he who had you. . . . That's not what's important. Explain to me why you kept quiet."

"I'd like to have it explained to *me*."

For a while we didn't speak. Menalcas, who was walking up and down the room, absentmindedly lit a cigarette, then threw it away at once.

"My dear Michel," he continued, "there is a 'sense,' as the others call it, a 'sense' that you seem to be lacking."

"The 'sense of morality,' perhaps," I said, making an effort to smile.

"Oh, no! Merely that of property."

"You don't seem to me to have much of it yourself."

"I have so little of it that, as you can see, nothing here belongs to me; not even, or rather especially not, the bed I sleep in. I can't stand repose; possession encourages it and in that feeling of security you fall asleep; I like living so much that I wish to spend my life awake and, therefore, in the very midst of my riches, I maintain that feeling of a precarious state by means of which I push my sensation of life to an extreme, or at least increase it. I can't say that I love danger, but I like a hazardous life and I want life to exact from me, at every moment, all my courage, all my happiness and all my health. . . ."

"Then, what are you blaming me for?" I interrupted.

"Oh, how you misunderstand me, my dear Michel; for once that I have the folly of trying to profess my faith! . . . If, Michel, I care very little about the approval or disapproval of mankind, it isn't so that I can go about approving or disapproving in my turn; those words don't have much meaning for me. I spoke far too much about myself just now; the idea of being understood carried me away. . . . I simply wanted to tell you that, for someone who doesn't have the sense of property, you seem to own a great deal of it; that's serious."

"What do I own that's all that great?"

"Nothing, if you take it that way. . . . But aren't you beginning your lecture course? Don't you have an estate in Normandy? Haven't you just moved into an apartment, and a luxurious one, in Passy? You're married. Aren't you expecting a child?"

"Well!" I said, losing my patience, "that simply proves that I've managed to create a life for myself that's more 'dangerous' than yours, to use your expression."

"Yes, simply that," Menalcas repeated with irony; then, turning sharply and giving me his hand, he said:

"All right, goodbye; that's enough for this evening, and we wouldn't get any further if we continued. But I hope to see you soon."

For some time I didn't see him again.

*　*　*

I was busy with new cares and new worries; an Italian scholar informed me of new documents he had brought to light, and I studied
them extensively for my course. The lack of comprehension that
greeted my first lecture had spurred my desire to throw a different and
much stronger light on those to follow; I was thereby led to formulate
as a doctrine what I had at first merely proposed as an ingenious hy-
pothesis. How many staunch proponents of a dogma owe their strength
to the good luck of being misunderstood when they merely hinted at
it! As for me, I admit I can't tell how much stubbornness may have
been mingled with my natural need to assert my beliefs. The novelty of what I had to say seemed all the more urgent to me in pro-
portion to the difficulty I had in saying it, and especially in getting it
heard.

But unfortunately, how pale the phrases became when compared to
actions! Wasn't Menalcas' life, his slightest gesture, a thousand times
more eloquent than my course? Oh, how well I understood, from then
on, that the almost exclusively ethical teachings of the great ancient philosophers were based as much, if not more, on what they did as on what
they said!

It was at my home that I saw Menalcas next, nearly three weeks after
our first meeting. It was near the end of a too heavily attended gathering. To avoid being disturbed daily, Marceline and I preferred to leave
our doors wide open on Thursday evenings, thus shutting them all the
more easily on other days. So that every Thursday we were visited by
those who called themselves our friends; the spaciousness of our parlors
allowed us to receive a large number of them, and the gathering lasted
far into the night. I think they were attracted above all by Marceline's
exquisite grace and the pleasure of talking to one another, because, beginning with the second of those evenings, I myself found nothing more
I wanted to hear or say, and didn't take much trouble to hide my boredom. I would roam from the smoking room to the parlor, from the ante-
room to the library, sometimes caught up by some phrase, not observing
much but casting almost random glances.

Antoine, Étienne and Godefroy were discussing the latest vote in
the Chamber of Deputies as they sprawled out on my wife's dainty
armchairs. Hubert and Louis were handling carelessly, and creasing,
wonderful etchings from my father's collection. In the smoking room,
Mathias, to pay better attention to Léonard, had put down his lit cigar
on a rosewood table. A glass of curaçao had been spilled on the carpet.
Albert was rudely stretched out on a couch, his muddy feet dirtying the
fabric. And the dust we were inhaling was composed of the terrible wear

and tear on everything. . . . I was seized with a furious desire to push all my guests out by their shoulders. Furniture, fabrics, prints lost all value for me at the least stain: blemished things, things tainted by illness and singled out for death. I would have liked to protect them all, keep them all under lock and key for myself alone. "How happy Menalcas is," I thought, "possessing nothing! *I* suffer because I want to preserve things. After all, what does all this matter to me? . . ."

In a small parlor that was less brightly illuminated and closed off by a panel of clear glass, Marceline was receiving a very few intimate friends; she was semirecumbent, resting on cushions; she was terribly pale, and seemed to me so tired that I was suddenly frightened by it and swore to myself that that reception would be the last. It was already late. I was going to look at my watch to check the time, when I felt Moktir's little scissors in my vest pocket.

"Then, why had he stolen them if he was going to ruin them, to destroy them immediately?" At that moment someone tapped me on the shoulder; I turned around sharply: it was Menalcas.

He was almost the only man in evening dress. He had just arrived. He asked me to introduce him to my wife; I surely wouldn't have done so of my own accord. Menalcas was elegant, almost handsome; an enormous drooping mustache, already gray, bisected his pirate's face; the cold flame in his eyes suggested courage and determination rather than kindness. No sooner was he in front of Marceline than I realized she didn't like him. After he had exchanged a few routine courteous phrases with her, I dragged him away into the smoking room.

That very morning I had learned of the new mission being entrusted to him by the Ministry of Colonies; various newspapers, responding to that news by recounting his adventurous career, seemed to have forgotten their vile insults of the recent past, and couldn't find terms striking enough in his praise. They rivaled one another in exaggerating the services rendered to our nation and to all of mankind by the strange discoveries he had made during his latest explorations, just as if everything he undertook had only a humanitarian aim; they boasted about his accustomed self-sacrifice, dedication and boldness just as if they expected him to find a reward in those praises.

I began to congratulate him; at my very first words he interrupted me:

"What! You, too, my dear Michel? And yet *you* hadn't insulted me beforehand," he said. "Leave that foolishness to the newspapers. They seem surprised today that a man of reproachable morals can still possess a few virtues. I can't find in myself the good and bad points they claim to discover; I exist only as a whole. I seek only what is natural, and, for each thing I do, the pleasure it gives me tells me that I was right to do it."

"That can take you far," I said.

"I'm counting on it," Menalcas replied. "Oh, if only everyone around us could be convinced of that! But most of them think they can't derive anything good from themselves except by constraint; they're only satisfied with themselves when they're disguised. Each one strives to resemble himself least of all. Each one chooses a pattern, then imitates it; in fact, they don't even choose the pattern they imitate, they accept one that's already chosen. And yet, I think, other things can be read in man. No one dares to. They don't dare to turn the page. Laws of imitation; I call them laws of fear. People are afraid of finding themselves alone, and they don't find themselves at all. This moral agoraphobia is hateful to me; it's the worst kind of cowardice. And yet it is only when alone that people are inventive. But who here is trying to be inventive? Whatever a man feels to be different in himself is precisely the rare thing he possesses, the thing that constitutes each man's worth — and it's that very thing they try to eradicate. They imitate. And they claim to love life!"

At first I let Menalcas talk; what he was saying was precisely what I had been saying to Marceline a month earlier, and so I should have approved it. Why, and through what cowardice, did I interrupt him and say to him, in imitation of Marceline, the very sentence, word for word, with which she had interrupted me then? — "But, my dear Menalcas, you can't expect each of them to be different from all the rest. . . ."

Menalcas fell silent abruptly, looked at me in an odd way, then, just as Eusebius was coming over to say good night to me, he turned his back on me rudely and went over to talk to Hector about trivial things.

As soon as I had spoken that sentence, it had seemed stupid to me; and I was especially sorry because it could make Menalcas think that I felt myself attacked by that speech of his. It was late; my guests were leaving. When the parlor was nearly empty, Menalcas came back over to me and said:

"I can't leave you like this. I must surely have misunderstood what you were saying. Let me at least hope so. . . ."

"No," I replied. "You didn't misunderstand me . . . but what I said made no sense; and as soon as I had said it, I began to suffer from its foolishness — and especially to feel that in your eyes it would place me among those very people whom you were just finding fault with, those who, I assure you, are as hateful to me as they are to you. I detest all principled people."

Laughing, Menalcas continued: "They're the most detestable thing in the world. No kind of sincerity can be expected of them, because they do only what their principles have decreed they had to do; otherwise they regard their actions as incorrect. At the mere suspicion that you could be of their party, I felt my words freeze on my lips. The sorrow I immediately felt revealed to me how strong my affection for you is; I wished I had been mistaken — not in my affection but in the judgment I was making."

"In fact, your judgment *was* wrong."

"Yes, wasn't it?" he said, suddenly taking my hand. "Listen; I have to leave soon, but I'd like to see you again. This time my trip will be longer and more dangerous than any of the others; I don't know when I'll be back. I must leave in two weeks; no one here knows that my departure is so imminent; I'm telling you this in secret. I leave at dawn. For me, each night before a departure is a night of terrible anguish. Prove to me that you aren't a man of principles; can I count on you to spend that last night with me?"

"But we'll see each other before then," I said, somewhat surprised.

"No. During these two weeks I'll no longer be at home to anyone; I won't even be in Paris. Tomorrow I leave for Budapest; in six days I must be in Rome. Here and there I have friends whom I want to say goodbye to before leaving Europe. Another one is expecting me in Madrid."

"It's understood, I'll spend that night of vigil with you."

"And we'll drink wine from Shiraz."

A few days after that gathering, Marceline's health took a turn for the worse. I've already said that she was frequently tired; but she would never complain of it, and, since I attributed that fatigue to her condition, I thought it was natural and refused to worry about it. An old doctor, rather foolish or inadequately informed, had at first given us excessive reassurances. But new spells of sickness, accompanied by fever, made me decide to call in Dr. Tr., who was then considered the most knowledgeable specialist. He was surprised that I hadn't called him sooner, and he prescribed a strict regimen which she should have been following for some time. Through a very imprudent bravery, Marceline had overtaxed her strength up till then; until her confinement, which was due toward the end of January, she was to spend her days on her chaise longue. Surely a little worried and suffering more than she was willing to admit, Marceline complied very amiably with the doctor's most inconvenient instructions. Nevertheless, she rebelled briefly when Tr. prescribed quinine for her in doses that she knew might be harmful to her child. For three days she stubbornly refused to take any; then, as her fever rose, she had to submit to that, too; but this time it was with great sadness and as if painfully renouncing the future; a sort of religious resignation snapped the willpower that had sustained

her until then, so that her condition suddenly worsened in the following few days.

I became even more attentive to her and comforted her to the best
of my ability, using Tr.'s own words (he saw nothing very serious in her
condition); but the violence of her fears finally alarmed me as well.
Oh, how dangerously our happiness was already basing itself on hopes
and on an uncertain future! I, who earlier had no taste for anything but
the past, had myself one day become tipsy with the unfamiliar savor of
the fleeting moment, I thought; but the future disenchants the present
even more than the present has disenchanted the past; and since our
night in Sorrento, all my love and all my life were oriented toward the
future.

Meanwhile the night came that I had promised to Menalcas; and despite my vexation at abandoning Marceline for a whole winter night, I
did my best to make her accept the solemnity of the appointment, the
gravity of my promise. Marceline was feeling a little better that evening,
and yet I was uneasy; a nurse took my place beside her. But, as soon as
I was in the street, my uneasiness increased in strength; I repressed it,
fought against it, annoyed with myself for being unable to free myself
of it altogether. Thus I gradually worked myself up into a state of hyper-
tension and unusual excitation, very different but at the same time very
close to the painful uneasiness that had given rise to it, but closer yet
to happiness. It was late; I was striding along; the snow started to fall
heavily; I was glad to breathe a keener air at last, to fight against the cold,
happy to confront the wind, the night, the snow; I savored my energy.

Menalcas, who heard me coming, appeared on the staircase landing.
He had been awaiting me impatiently. He was pale and seemed a bit
edgy. He took my coat and forced me to exchange my wet boots for soft
Persian slippers. On an end table near the fire were some snacks. Two
lamps illuminated the room, but less than the fireplace did. At the very
outset Menalcas inquired after Marceline's health; to simplify matters,
I answered that she was feeling very well.

"You're expecting your child soon?" he went on.

"In a month."

Menalcas leaned over toward the fire as if he wanted to hide his face.
He was silent. He kept silent so long that I was finally quite embarrassed,
not knowing what else to say to him. I stood up, took a few steps, then,
going up to him, placed my hand on his shoulder. Then, as if continuing
his train of thought, he murmured:

"One must choose. The important thing is knowing what you
want. . . ."

"Oh! You no longer wish to take this trip?" I asked him, unsure of the meaning I was to glean from his words.

"It looks that way."

"Are you hesitant, then?"

"What for? You, who have a wife and child, are staying here. . . . Of the thousand forms of life each man can know only one. To envy the happiness of others is folly; you wouldn't know how to make use of it. Happiness shouldn't come ready made, but should be custom made. I'm leaving tomorrow; I know that I've tried to cut this happiness to my own measure. . . . Hold onto your peaceful domestic happiness. . . ."

"*I* had cut my happiness to my own measure, too," I exclaimed; "but I've grown; now my happiness is too tight on me; sometimes I'm almost strangled by it. . . ."

"Bah! You'll get used to it!" said Menalcas; then he planted himself in front of me, stared into my eyes and, when I found nothing to say, he smiled a little sadly. "A man thinks he owns things, and it's he who is owned," he continued. "Pour yourself some Shiraz, my dear Michel; you won't get to taste it often; and eat some of those pink candies the Persians take with it. For this evening I'll drink with you, I'll forget that I'm leaving tomorrow, and I'll chat as if this were a long night. . . . Do you know what makes dead letters of poetry and especially philosophy today? It's because they're detached from life. Greece created idealism directly out of living reality; so that an artist's life was already a poetic accomplishment in itself; a philosopher's life was an activation of his philosophy; so that, in addition, mingling with life instead of being unaware of one another, philosophy nourished poetry, poetry expressed philosophy, and they had remarkable powers of persuasion. Today beauty no longer acts; action is no longer concerned with being beautiful; and wisdom operates on its own."

"Why," I said, "don't you, who live out your wisdom, write your memoirs? Or simply," I went on, seeing him smile, "the recollections of your travels?"

"Because I don't want to recollect them," he replied. "If I did that, I would think I was preventing the future from arriving and making the past encroach on it. I create the newness of each hour by completely forgetting yesterday. To have *been* happy is never enough for me. I don't believe in dead things, and, in my mind, to exist no longer is the same as never having existed."

At length I was annoyed at that speech, which was too far in advance of my own thinking; I would have liked to pull back, to stop him; but I strove in vain to contradict; besides, I was even more annoyed with myself than with Menalcas. And so I remained silent. As for him, now he would walk back and forth like a caged animal, now he would lean over to the fire, now he would be silent for a long while, then all at once he said:

"If our mediocre brains only knew how to embalm their memories! But our memories are hard to keep fresh; the most delicate ones are stripped bare, the most voluptuous ones rot away; the most delightful ones are the most dangerous later on. Those you regret were delightful at the start."

Again, a long silence; and then he resumed:

"Regrets, remorse, repentance are joys of the past seen from behind. I don't like to look back, and I leave my past far behind me just as birds leave their cool shade so they can fly away. Oh, Michel, every joy always awaits us, but always wants to find an empty bed, to be the only one; it wants you to come to it like a widower. Oh, Michel, all joy is like that manna in the desert which spoils from one day to the next; it's like the water of the spring Ameles which Plato tells us couldn't be kept in any container. . . . Let each instant take away everything it had brought."

Menalcas went on talking for some time; I can't quote all his phrases here, but many of them were burnt into my mind, and those I would have liked to forget most quickly penetrated most deeply; not that they taught me anything brand-new — but they suddenly laid bare my own thoughts, thoughts that I had been covering with so many veils that I had almost been able to hope they were stifled. That is how our vigil was spent.

When, in the morning, after escorting Menalcas to the train that carried him away, I set out alone to return home to Marceline, I felt full of a loathsome sadness, of hatred for Menalcas' cynical joy; I wanted to find it artificial; I strove to deny it. I was annoyed at having been unable to rebut it; I was annoyed at having made some remarks that could lead him to doubt my happiness, my love. And I clutched at my dubious happiness, "my peaceful happiness," as Menalcas called it; unfortunately I couldn't suppress my uneasiness over it, but I insisted that this uneasiness served as a nourishment for love. I looked into the future, already seeing my little child smiling at me; for his sake my morality was being reshaped and fortified. . . . Decidedly I was walking with firm steps.

Unfortunately, when I got home that morning, an unaccustomed disorder struck me in the very first room. The nurse came to meet me and informed me, in guarded terms, that my wife had been a prey to terrible anguish during the night, then had felt strong pains, although she didn't think the time for delivery had come yet; that, feeling very poorly, she had sent for the doctor; that the doctor, although he had arrived hastily during the night, had not yet left his patient. Then, I think because she saw how pale I was, she tried to reassure me, saying that everything was much better now, that . . . I hastened toward Marceline's room.

The room was only partially illuminated, and at first I could only make out the doctor, who signaled to me to keep silent; then, in the darkness, a figure I didn't know. Anxiously, noiselessly, I went up to the bed. Marceline had her eyes closed; she was so terribly pale that at first I thought she was dead, but, without opening her eyes, she turned her head in my direction. In a dark corner of the room, the unknown figure was putting away and hiding various objects; I saw gleaming instruments, absorbent cotton; I saw, or thought I saw, a blood-stained cloth. . . . I felt myself tottering; I almost fell onto the doctor; he supported me. I understood; I was afraid to understand. . . .

"The little one?" I asked anxiously.

He shrugged his shoulders sadly. No longer knowing what I was doing, I threw myself against the bed, sobbing. Oh, that sudden future! All at once the ground gave way under my feet; before me there was nothing but an empty hole into which I stumbled and was swallowed up.

Here everything becomes confused in a shadowy memory. And yet at first Marceline seemed to recover quickly. The New Year vacation gave me a little respite and I was able to spend almost my full day with her. At her side, I would read, write or read aloud to her softly. I almost never went out without bringing her back some flowers. I recalled the tender care she had lavished on me when I was the sick one, and I lavished so much love on her that it sometimes made her smile, as if she were happy. Not a word was exchanged on the subject of that sad accident which slaughtered our hopes. . . .

Then phlebitis set in, and, when it started to wear off, a blood clot suddenly brought Marceline to the brink of death. It was nighttime; I can still see myself bending over her, feeling my own heart stop or revive along with hers. How many nights I watched over her that way! My eyes obstinately fixed on her, hoping, through the strength of my love, to infuse a little of my life into hers. And if I no longer thought a great deal about happiness, my only sad joy was to see Marceline sometimes smile.

My course had resumed. Where did I find the strength to prepare my lectures and to deliver them? . . . My memories are lost and I don't know how those weeks went by. And yet I'd like to tell you about one little incident:

It was one morning shortly after the blood clot; I was there with

Marceline; she seemed a little better, but she was still under orders to lie as still as possible; she wasn't even supposed to move her arms. I was leaning over her to give her a drink and, after she had taken it and I was still bent over her, she asked me, in a voice made even weaker by her agitation, to open a little box that she pointed out with her eyes. The box was there on the table; I opened it; it was full of ribbons, shreds of cloths, little jewels not worth anything; what did she want? I brought the box over to the bed; I took out each object one by one. Was it this? That? No, not yet; I sensed that she was getting a little worried. "Oh, Marceline, it's the little rosary you want!" She made an effort to smile.

"So you're afraid I'm not taking good enough care of you?"

"Oh, darling!" she murmured. And I remembered our conversation in Biskra, her fearful reproach when she heard me reject what she called "the help of God." I continued somewhat roughly:

"I did get better all on my own."

"I prayed so hard for you," she replied. She said that tenderly, sadly; I felt a beseeching anxiety in her eyes. . . . I took the rosary and slipped it into her weakened hand that was resting on the sheet alongside her. A glance laden with tears and love was my reward — but I couldn't respond to it; I lingered another moment, not knowing what to do, remaining there in embarrassment; finally, unable to stand it any more, I said "Goodbye" to her — and left the room, hostile, as if I had been driven out of it.

Meanwhile the blood clot had generated a very serious condition; the terrible clot that her heart had ejected wearied and congested her lungs and obstructed her breathing, making it difficult and causing her to wheeze. I thought I'd never see her better again. Sickness had entered into Marceline, inhabited her from then on, singled her out, blemished her. She was a damaged thing.

III

The season was becoming mild. As soon as my course was over, I brought Marceline to La Morinière, since the doctor assured us that there was no longer any immediate danger and that, to restore her completely, nothing would be more beneficial than fresher air. I myself had a great need of rest. Those wakeful nights I had had to put in almost entirely on my own, that prolonged worry, and especially that kind of physical sympathy which, at the time of Marceline's blood clot, had made me feel the terrible throbbing of her heart within myself, all that had tired me out as if I had been ill myself.

I would have preferred to take Marceline to the mountains; but she made plain to me the keenest desire to return to Normandy, insisting that no climate would be better for her, and reminding me that I had to go back to those two farms with which I had somewhat rashly burdened myself. She convinced me that I had made myself responsible for them and that I owed it to myself to make a go of them. And so we had scarcely arrived when she urged me to visit the grounds. . . . I'm not sure whether her friendly insistence didn't entail a great deal of self-sacrifice: the fear that, otherwise, I might feel tied down to her by the attentions she still needed and wouldn't seem sufficiently free. . . . But Marceline was feeling better; the blush was back in her cheeks; and nothing relaxed me more than to feel that her smile was less sad; I was able to leave her alone without fear.

And so I went back to the farms. Haymaking was beginning there. The air, laden with pollen and fragrances, dizzied me at the outset like a heady beverage. I felt as if, ever since the year before, I had no longer breathed, or else had inhaled only dust, so soothingly did the atmosphere penetrate me. From the slope on which I was seated, as if tipsy, I had an overview of La Morinière; I saw its blue roofs, the still waters of its moats; around it, mown fields, others still grassy; farther away, the bend in the stream; even farther, woods in which I had ridden with Charles the preceding autumn. The singing I had heard for a few moments drew nearer; it was haymakers returning, their pitchfork or rake on their shoulders. These farmhands, almost all of whom I recognized, made me remember regretfully that I wasn't there as a fascinated tourist but as the master. I went up to them, smiled at them, spoke to them, asked news of each one at length. Already that morning Bocage had been able to report to me on the condition of the crops; furthermore, in a steady stream of letters he hadn't ceased to inform me about the slightest incidents concerning the farms. Work on them wasn't going badly, much better than Bocage had at first led me to hope. And yet I had been awaited for some important decisions and, for a few days, I supervised everything to the best of my ability, without pleasure, but propping up my shattered life with that semblance of work.

As soon as Marceline was well enough to have guests, some friends came to live with us. Their company, affectionate and easy on the nerves, was pleasant for Marceline, but made me leave the house all the more readily. I preferred the company of the farmhands; I felt that with them I could learn more — not that I asked them many questions — and I can hardly express the kind of happiness I felt when with them. I seemed to be feeling things through their agency — and, whereas the conversation of our friends was already overfamiliar to me even before they started speaking, the mere sight of those vagabonds amazed me continually.

If at first it could truly be said that, when replying to me, they showed all the condescendence that I *avoided* showing when questioning them, soon they were more tolerant of my presence. I got in closer and closer touch with them. Not content with following them around while they worked, I wanted to see them at play; their dull minds hardly interested me, but I shared their meals, listened to their jokes and lovingly observed their pleasures. It was a kind of sympathetic vibration, like the one that made my heart throb along with Marceline's; it was a direct echo of every unfamiliar sensation — not at all vague, but precise, sharp. I felt the mower's aches and pains in my own arms; I grew weary along with his weariness; the mouthful of cider he swallowed quenched my thirst; I felt it glide down his throat; one day, while sharpening his scythe, one of them cut deeply into his thumb; I felt his pain, to the very bone.

Thus, it seemed to me that it was not my eyesight alone that taught me the countryside, but that I also felt it through a sort of physical contact, which this strange sympathy made boundless.

Bocage's presence bothered me; whenever he came by, I had to play the role of master, and I no longer found any pleasure in it. I was still giving orders — I had to — and was supervising the workers in my way; but I no longer rode on horseback, for fear of towering over them too much. But, despite the precautions I took so they would no longer suffer from my presence and would feel no more constraint before me, I remained full of morbid curiosity about them, as before. The existence of each one of them was still a mystery to me. I always felt that some part of their life was hidden from me. What did they do when I wasn't there? I wouldn't accept the fact that they might be having a better time. And I ascribed to each of them a secret that I stubbornly wanted to know. I prowled around them, I followed them, I spied on them. I would try to get close to the most simple-minded characters among them, as if I expected their mental darkness to shed some light on the mystery.

One of them, especially, attracted me; he was quite good-looking, tall, not at all stupid, but guided solely by instinct; everything he did was done on the spur of the moment, and he gave in to every passing impulse. He wasn't from that area; he had been hired by chance. An excellent worker for two days, he would be dead drunk on the third. One night I went furtively to see him in the barn; he was sprawled in the hay; he was sleeping a heavy drunken sleep. How long I looked at him! . . . One fine day he left just as he had come. I would have liked to know by what route. . . . That very evening I learned that Bocage had discharged him.

I was furious with Bocage; I sent for him.

"It seems you've discharged Pierre," I began. "Would you like to tell me why?"

Somewhat taken aback by my anger, which I was nonetheless controlling as best I could, he said:

"Sir, you didn't want to keep on such a dirty drunk, who was corrupting the best workers . . ."

"I know better than you whom I want to keep."

"A tramp! No one even knows where he came from. That was causing bad blood in the area. . . . Maybe if he had set fire to the barn one night, you would have been satisfied."

"But, after all, that's my business, and the farm is mine, I imagine; I intend to run it the way I like. In the future, please inform me of your motives before firing anybody."

Bocage, as I've said, had known me when I was very young; no matter how wounding the tone of my speech was, he liked me too well to get very angry at it. What's more, he didn't take me seriously enough. A Norman peasant all too often refuses to believe anything he can't grasp the reason for; that is, anything that doesn't profit him. Bocage considered that argument simply as a quirk.

And yet I didn't want to break off our talk on a note of reproach, and, feeling that I had been too abrasive, I stopped to think about something to add.

"Shouldn't your son Charles be coming back soon?" I decided to ask after a moment of silence.

"I thought you had forgotten about him, sir, seeing how little you were concerned with him," said Bocage, still hurt.

"I, forget him! Bocage, how could I, after all we did together last year? In fact, I'm counting on him a great deal for those farms. . . ."

"Very kind, sir. Charles should be back in a week."

"Good, I'm glad to hear it, Bocage" — and I sent him away.

Bocage was nearly right; of course, I hadn't forgotten Charles, but

I was no longer very concerned about him. How can I explain that, after so ardent a friendship, I no longer felt anything but a fretful lack of curiosity regarding him? It was because my occupations and tastes were no longer those of the year before. I had to admit to myself that my two farms no longer interested me as much as the people I employed on them; and if I were to spend time with them, the presence of Charles would be a nuisance. He was much too logical and demanded too much respect. And so, despite the strong emotion his memory aroused in me, it was with fear that I saw his return approaching.

He came back. Oh, how right I was to be afraid, and how properly Menalcas acted in rejecting all memories! In place of Charles, I saw a ridiculous gentleman walk in, wearing a silly derby hat. God, how he had changed! Embarrassed, constrained, I nevertheless tried not to show too much coldness in response to the joy he showed at seeing me again; but I disliked even that joy; it was clumsy and struck me as insincere. I had received him in the parlor, and, since it was late, I couldn't make out his face too clearly; but when a lamp was brought in, I saw with disgust that he had let his side whiskers grow.

Our conversation that evening was rather dismal; then, since I knew he would be on the farms constantly, I avoided going there for nearly a week, falling back on my studies and the company of my guests. Then, as soon as I started going out again, a very new order of business demanded my attention.

Woodcutters had invaded the woods. Every year a part of the forest was sold; divided into twelve equal cutting areas, each year it provided a twelve years' growth of underbrush to be chopped into firewood, along with a few saplings that were no longer expected to grow.

This work was done in the winter; then, before spring, according to the deed of sale, the woodcutters were to have cleared the cutting area. But the negligence of old man Heurtevent, the wood dealer who ran the operation, was so great that sometimes springtime found the area still grown over; then fragile new shoots could be seen stretching out through the dead branches, and when the woodcutters finally removed the lumber, they couldn't help ruining many buds.

That year the carelessness of old man Heurtevent, the buyer, surpassed our worst expectations. Since there was no higher bid, I had had to grant him the cutting contract at a very low price; thus, sure of making out all right no matter what he did, he was in no hurry to clear the section of forest for which he had paid so little. And from week to week he put off the work, now blaming the delay on a lack of manpower, now on bad weather, then on a sick horse, unavoidable duties elsewhere, other jobs . . . anything. So that in the middle of the summer nothing had yet been removed.

A state of affairs that, the year before, would have tried my patience to the utmost, this year left me quite calm; I didn't deceive myself as to the harm Heurtevent was doing me; but those woods, ravaged that way, were beautiful, and I strolled through them with pleasure, looking around, observing the game, startling the snakes, and sometimes sitting for long stretches on one of the recumbent trunks that seemed still alive and was still emitting a few green sprigs from its wounds.

Then, suddenly, toward the middle of the first half of August, Heurtevent decided to send his men. They came six at a time, claiming they would finish the whole job in ten days. The part of the forest being cleared was nearly adjacent to La Valterie; to make the woodcutters' work easier, I consented to having their meals brought from that farm. The man assigned to that task was a joker named Bute, who had just returned from his military service rotten to the core — I mean, in mind; his body was in great shape. He was one of those employees of mine with whom I liked to chat. And so this way I could see him without making a special trip to the farm. Because it was exactly at that time that I started going out again. And for a few days I hardly left the woods, returning to La Morinière only at mealtime, and often keeping the others waiting. I pretended to be supervising the work, but I was really just visiting the workmen.

Sometimes this gang of six men was joined by two of Heurtevent's sons, one twenty, the other fifteen, both of them lean, with deeply incurved backs, with hard features. They looked foreign, and, in fact, I learned later on that their mother was Spanish. At first I was surprised that she could have come all that way, but it seems that Heurtevent, a confirmed rover as a young man, had married her in Spain. For that reason he was not much liked in the neighborhood. The first time I had met the younger son, as I recall, was in the rain; he was alone, sitting on a very high wagon at the very top of a heap of firewood; and there, stretched out on his back among the branches, he was singing, rather howling, a kind of bizarre chant such as I had never heard in that region. The horses that were pulling the wagon knew the road and were proceeding without any guidance. I can't tell you what an effect that chant had on me, because I had only heard its like in Africa. . . . The boy, excited, seemed drunk; when I passed by he didn't even look at me. The next day I learned he was a son of Heurtevent. It was to see him again, or at least to await him, that I lingered in the cutting area

that way. It was soon cleared. The Heurtevent boys came there only
three times. They seemed stuck up, and I couldn't get a word out of
them.

Bute, on the other hand, enjoyed telling stories; I soon gave him to
understand just how freely he could talk in my presence; from then
on he had no qualms and laid the neighborhood bare. I avidly investigated his mystery. At one and the same time, he outdid my expectations and failed to satisfy me. Was that what was lurking beneath the
outward appearances? Or, rather, was this only more hypocrisy? What
did it matter! And I went on questioning Bute, as I had questioned the
crude chronicles of the Goths. His narratives emitted a troubled vapor
from the abyss which was already going to my head and which I was
inhaling with anxiety. Through him I first learned that Heurtevent was
sleeping with his own daughter. I feared that, if I showed the slightest
reproach, all his confidences would be cut short; so I smiled; curiosity
led me on.

"And her mother? She says nothing?"

"Her mother! It's a good twelve years since she died. . . . He used to
beat her."

"How many are there in the family?"

"Five children. You've seen the eldest and the youngest sons. There's
another one who's sixteen; he's not strong and he wants to become a
priest. And then the older daughter already has two children by her
father. . . ."

And gradually I learned many other things which turned the
Heurtevent household into a place of hellfire with a strong stench; and
no matter what I might say, my imagination kept circling around it like
a blowfly. One evening the eldest son tried to rape a young maidservant;
and while she was resisting him, his father came along and helped him,
holding her still with his enormous hands; all this time the second son,
on the floor above, was tenderly continuing to pray, and the youngest
one, a witness to the action, was enjoying himself. As for the rape, I
imagine that it hadn't been difficult, because Bute went on to tell that, not
long afterward, the maid, who had begun to like it, had tried to seduce
the little priest.

"And her attempt didn't succeed?" I asked.

"He's still holding out, but not very staunchly any more," Bute replied.

"Didn't you say there was another daughter?"

"Who takes on all comers; and doesn't even ask for pay. When she
gets the urge, she would even pay for it herself. But it's dangerous to

sleep with her at her father's place; he'd beat you up. His motto is that at home you've got the right to do whatever you like, but that it's no business of anybody else's. Pierre, the farmhand you discharged, didn't go around bragging about it, but one night he didn't get out of there without a hole in his head. Since then, she has her fun in the manor-house woods."

And then, with an encouraging look, I asked: "Have you tried?"

He lowered his eyes for form's sake and said, laughing: "Occasionally." And then, quickly lifting his eyes: "Old man Bocage's kid, too."

"Old man Bocage's kid? Which one?"

"Alcide, the one who sleeps on the farm. You don't know him, then?" I was completely thunderstruck to learn that Bocage had another son. "It's true," Bute continued, "that last year he was still at his uncle's. But it's really surprising that you haven't met him yet in the woods; he goes poaching almost every night."

Bute had spoken those last words in a lower tone. He looked hard at me and I realized I had to smile. Then, contented, Bute went on:

"Of course you're damn well aware that poaching goes on there. Bah! The woods are so big that it doesn't do much harm."

I showed so little annoyance that, very quickly, Bute, emboldened and, as I see it today, happy to do Bocage a bad turn, showed me some snares set by Alcide in a hollow, then showed me a spot in the hedge where I could be almost sure of surprising him. It was a narrow opening in the border hedge at the the top of a slope, through which Alcide was accustomed to slip around six o'clock. There Bute and I, greatly entertained, spanned a copper wire, very adroitly camouflaged. Then, making me swear that I wouldn't give him away, Bute left, unwilling to compromise himself. I lay down against the far side of the slope; I waited.

And for three evenings I waited in vain. I was beginning to think that Bute had fooled me. . . . Finally, on the fourth evening, I heard very light footsteps approaching. My heart was beating and I suddenly learned the terrible, deep pleasure of the poacher. . . . The snare was so well set that Alcide walked right into it. I saw him suddenly go sprawling, his ankle caught. He tried to escape, fell down again, and thrashed around like a game animal. But I already had hold of him. He was a spiteful urchin, with green eyes, towlike hair and a shifty expression. He kicked out at me; then, when immobilized, tried to bite me; when he was unable to do so, he poured out a stream of the most remarkable curses I had ever heard up to that time. Finally I couldn't control myself; I burst out laughing. Then he suddenly stopped, looked at me and said, in a lower tone: "You damn beast, you've crippled me."

"Show me."

He slipped his stocking down over his clog and showed me his ankle, where I could just barely make out a slight pinkish mark. "That's nothing." He smiled a little, then said craftily:

"I'm gonna tell my father it's you that's setting the snares."

"Hell! It's one of yours."

"I'm sure it wasn't you who set that one!"

"Why not?"

"You couldn't do such a good job. Show me how you go about it."

"Teach me. . . ."

That evening I was very late for dinner and, since no one knew where I was, Marceline was worried. But I didn't tell her that I had set six snares and that, far from scolding Alcide, I had given him ten sous.

The next day, going out to check up on those snares with him, I was amused to find two rabbits that had been trapped; naturally I turned them over to him. Hunting season hadn't opened yet. So what became of that game, which you couldn't show anyone without implicating yourself? That's what Alcide refused to confess to me. Finally I found out, again through Bute, that Heurtevent was a past master at receiving stolen goods, and that his youngest son played the middleman between Alcide and him. Was I, then, in this way to penetrate more of the secrets of that antisocial family? With what passion I went on poaching!

I met Alcide every evening; we caught a large number of rabbits, and once even a roedeer; it still had a little life in it. It is only with horror that I recall the joy with which Alcide killed it. We put the deer in a safe place where the Heurtevent boy could come to get it during the night.

From then on, I didn't go out so often in the daytime, when the bare patches of woodland were less attractive to me. I even tried to work; unhappy, aimless work — because as soon as my course was over I had refused to resume my temporary employment — thankless work, from which I was distracted by the slightest snatch of song, the slightest noise in the countryside; every shout called out to me to come. How many times I thus jumped up from my reading and raced to my window, only to see nothing at all going on! How many times, going out suddenly . . . The only thing to which I was able to pay attention was all my senses.

But when night fell — and at that season, it already fell early — it was our time, the beauty of which I hadn't imagined before then; and I would go out the way burglars break in. I had acquired a night bird's eyes. I marveled at the grass, which stirred more briskly and seemed higher, at the trees with their denser foliage. The night hollowed out everything, made it more remote, made the ground distant and every surface deep. The most level path seemed dangerous. All around you could feel the awakening of each thing that leads a shadowy existence.

"Where does your father think you are now?"

"Watching the livestock in the cowshed."

Alcide used to sleep there, I knew, right near the pigeons and chickens; since he was locked in at evening, he would get out through a hole in the roof; his clothes retained a warm odor of poultry. . . .

Then, brusquely, as soon as the game was collected, he would disappear into the night as if through a trapdoor, without a farewell gesture, without even saying "See you tomorrow." I knew that before going home to the farm, where the dogs made no noise at his arrival, he would go to meet the Heurtevent boy and hand over his catch to him. But where? That's what I couldn't detect, as much as I longed to; threats and ploys failed; the Heurtevents wouldn't let anyone get near them. And I don't know what indicated most clearly the triumph of my folly: the pursuit of a banal mystery that kept on eluding me, or perhaps the very creation of that mystery by my own curiosity? But what did Alcide do when he left me? Did he really sleep at the farm? Or did he only make the farmer think so? Oh, it did me no good to become his accomplice; the only result was losing more of his respect without gaining more of his confidence; and that infuriated me and distressed me at the same time. . . .

After his abrupt disappearances, I would feel terribly alone; and I would return home across the fields, through the grass heavy with dew, intoxicated with the night, primitive life and anarchy, soaked, muddy, covered with leaves. From afar, in sleeping La Morinière, I seemed to be guided, as by a tranquil lighthouse, by the lamp in Marceline's bedroom; I had convinced her that, if I didn't go out like that at night, I wouldn't be able to fall asleep. It was true: I conceived a loathing for my bed, and I would have preferred the barn.

Game was abundant that year. Rabbits, hares, pheasants succeeded one another. Seeing that everything was going as he wished, after three evenings Bute found pleasure in joining us.

On the sixth evening of poaching, we found only two of our twelve snares: there had been a raid during the day. Bute asked me for a hundred sous to buy more copper wire, since iron wire was worthless.

The next day I had the pleasure of seeing my ten snares at Bocage's place, and I had to compliment him on his zeal. To top it all, a year earlier I had unthinkingly promised a reward of ten sous for every snare confiscated, so I had to give Bocage a hundred. Meanwhile, with *his* hundred sous, Bute bought copper wire. Four days later, the same story: ten new snares confiscated. Again, a hundred sous to Bute; again, a hundred sous to Bocage. And when I congratulated him, he said:

"It's not me you should congratulate. It's Alcide."

"What!"

Too much surprise can undo us; I controlled myself.

"Yes," Bocage continued; "what would you have, sir? I'm getting old and I'm needed too much on the farm. The young one patrols the woods for me; he knows them; he's clever and he knows better than I do where to look for traps and locate them."

"I don't find that at all hard to believe, Bocage."

"Then, out of the ten sous you give me, I let him have five sous per trap."

"He certainly deserves it. Damn! Twenty snares in five days! He's done a good job. The poachers have gotten their due warning. They're going to relax, I wager."

"Oh, sir, the more we take the more we find. Game is selling at a high price this year, and for the few sous it costs them . . ."

I was so thoroughly tricked that I nearly thought Bocage was an accomplice. And what exasperated me about that matter wasn't Alcide's triple dealing, but seeing him deceive me like that. And, then, what were Bute and he doing with the money? "I don't know," I told myself; "I'll never know a thing about such creatures. They'll always lie; they'll deceive me just for the sake of doing so." That evening it wasn't a hundred sous but ten francs that I gave to Bute; I warned him that it was the last time and that, if the snares were confiscated again, that would be the end of it.

The next day I saw Bocage coming; he looked quite embarrassed; I immediately became more so than he. What had happened? Bocage informed me that Bute hadn't returned to the farm until the wee hours of the morning; Bute was drunk as a lord; at the first words Bocage addressed to him, Bute insulted him foully, then jumped on him and hit him. . . .

"Finally," Bocage said, "I came to know whether you authorize me" — he dwelled a moment on the phrase — "authorize me to discharge him."

"I'll think it over, Bocage. I'm very sorry he showed you disrespect. I see. . . . Let me think it over by myself; and come back here in two hours."

Bocage went out.

To keep Bute on would have meant withdrawing support from Bocage shamefully; to kick Bute out would have meant inciting him to revenge. Oh well! Come what may! After all, I was the only one to blame . . . And, as soon as Bocage came back, I said:

"You can tell Bute his presence is no longer desired here."

Then I waited. What was Bocage doing? What was Bute saying? It was only in the evening that I heard some repercussions of the scandal. Bute had talked. I understood it first from the cries I heard in Bocage's house; it was little Alcide being beaten. I knew Bocage would come; he did; I heard his elderly steps drawing near, and my heart beat even harder than it had beaten for the game. An intolerable moment! He would be justified in spouting every lofty sentiment; I would be forced to take him seriously. What excuses could I make up? What a bad job of acting I was going to do! Oh, I wanted to hand in my part in the play . . . Bocage came in. I understood literally nothing he said. It was absurd: I had to ask him to start all over again. Finally I made out this much: He thought Bute was the only guilty party; the incredible truth eluded him; he was too much of a Norman to admit that I gave ten francs to Bute (and to what purpose?). Bute surely stole those ten francs; by claiming I gave them to him, he was adding lying to robbery; it was an effort to cloak his theft; Bocage wasn't the man to be gulled by all that. . . . There was no further mention of poaching. If Bocage beat Alcide, it was because the youngster was sleeping outside.

Well, now! I was saved; in front of Bocage, at least, everything was all right. What a fool that Bute was! To be sure, I didn't much feel like poaching that evening.

I thought the incident was already closed, but an hour later Charles showed up. He didn't seem to be in a joking mood; even from a distance he looked like even more of a bore than his father. And to think that the year before . . .

"Well, Charles, it's been a while since I've seen you."

"If you really wanted to see me, all you had to do was come to the farm. I have no damn business with the woods or night hours."

"Oh, your father told you . . ."

"My father told me nothing because my father knows nothing. Why does he need to learn, at his age, that his master is making a damn fool of him?"

"Watch out, Charles! You're going too far . . ."

"Oh, hell! You're the master, and you do what you like!"

"Charles, you know perfectly well that I haven't made fun of anybody, and if I do what I like it's because it harms nobody but my-self."

He shrugged his shoulders slightly.

"How do you expect others to protect your interests when you attack them yourself? You can't patronize the gamekeeper and the poacher at the same time."

"Why not?"

"Because then . . . Ah! Look, sir, all this is too subtle for me, and I sim-ply don't like to see my master in cahoots with people who get arrested, helping them undo the work others have done for him."

And Charles said that in a tone that gradually increased in self-confidence. He conducted himself almost nobly. I noticed he had cut his whiskers. Besides, what he was saying was quite fair. And, since I kept silent (what could I say to him?), he continued:

"You yourself taught me last year that a man has duties toward his property, but you seem to have forgotten that. He's got to take those duties seriously and give up fooling around with them . . . or else he never deserved to have that property in the first place."

Silence.

"Is that all you had to say?"

"For tonight, yes, sir; but some other night, if you keep pressing me, I may come to tell you that my father and I are leaving La Morinière."

And he walked away, after making me a very low bow. I hardly took the time to think it over:

"Charles!" Damn it, he was right. . . . But if that's what you call be-ing an owner! . . . "Charles!" I ran after him; I caught up with him in the darkness, and said, very quickly, as if to put the seal on my sudden decision:

"You can inform your father that I'm putting La Morinière up for sale."

Charles bowed solemnly and walked off without a word.

All that was ridiculous.

That evening Marceline couldn't come down for dinner and sent word to me that she was ill. I went upstairs hastily and, full of anxiety, entered her room. She reassured me at once. "It's only a cold," she said, with hope in her voice. She had caught a chill.

"Couldn't you have put on something warm?"

"I did. The moment I started to shiver, I put on my shawl."

"You shouldn't have put it on after you were shivering, but before."

She looked at me, tried to smile. . . . Ah! Maybe a day that had begun so badly disposed me to anguish. If she had asked me out loud, "Are you really so eager for me to go on living?" I couldn't have understood her more clearly. Decidedly, everything was falling to pieces around me; no matter what my hand clutched at, it was unable to hold onto. . . . I ran over to Marceline and covered her pale temples with kisses. Then, she could no longer control herself and sobbed on my shoulder.

"Oh, Marceline, Marceline! Let's get away from here. In some other place, I'll love you the way I loved you in Sorrento. You thought I had changed, didn't you? But in some other place, you'll realize that nothing has changed our love. . . ."

My saying this was no cure yet for her sadness, but how she began already to grasp at hope!

The season wasn't far advanced, but it was damp and cold, and the last buds on the rosebushes were already rotting without being able to open. Our guests had left us for some time now. Marceline was not too ill to undertake the task of shutting up the house, and five days later we departed.

PART THREE

AND SO I tried once again to get a firm hold on my love. But what need had I for peaceful happiness? The happiness that Marceline gave me, and represented for me, was like repose to a man who doesn't feel tired. But since I realized that she was worn out and needed my love, I enveloped her in it and pretended that it was through my own need of it. I felt her suffering intensely; it was to cure her of it that I loved her.

Oh, passionate attentions! Tender vigils! Just as others reignite their religious faith by exaggerating its rituals, so I unfurled my love. And, I tell you, Marceline immediately reawakened to hope. There was still so much youth in her; so much promise in me, she thought. We escaped from Paris as if on a second honeymoon. But, from the very first day of the journey, she started feeling much worse; when we reached Neuchâtel we already had to stop.

How I loved that lake with its blue-green banks, with nothing alpine about it, whose waters, like those of a swamp, mingle with the earth for some time and seep through the reeds! In a very comfortable hotel I was able to find Marceline a room with a lake view; I stayed with her all day long.

She was feeling so poorly that, the very next day, I sent for a doctor from Lausanne. He was concerned, quite pointlessly, to find out whether I knew of any other cases of tuberculosis in my wife's family. I said I did, even though I really didn't; it was because I disliked saying that I myself had suffered from it and had almost been given up as a hopeless case; and that, before tending me, Marceline had never been ill. So I blamed everything on the blood clot, even though the doctor was unwilling to consider that as anything but a secondary cause, and assured me that the illness had been contracted earlier. He warmly recommended to us the fresh air of the high Alps, where he assured us

Marceline would get better; and since it was already my wish to spend the whole winter in the Engadine, we set out again as soon as Marceline was well enough to tolerate the journey.

I remember all my feelings along the way as if they were events. The weather was clear and cold; we had brought along the warmest furs. . . . At Chur, the uninterrupted noise at the hotel prevented us almost altogether from sleeping. I would gladly have accepted a sleepless night, which wouldn't have left me tired; but Marceline . . . And I wasn't so much upset by that noise as by her inability to fall asleep despite the noise. It would have been so good for her! The next day we left before dawn; we had reserved the compartment seats inside the Chur coach; the well-organized relays allow you to reach St. Moritz in a day.

Tiefencastel, the Piz Julier, Samedan . . . I remember everything, hour by hour; the very new quality and the inclemency of the air; the sound of the horses' bells; my hunger, the noon stop in front of the inn; the raw egg I broke into my soup, the dark bread and the coldness of the acrid wine. Those coarse foods were unsuitable for Marceline; the only thing she could eat was a few dry biscuits I had providentially thought to take along on the way. I recall the sunset, the rapid climbing of the shadows up the forested slopes; then another stop. The air became sharper and harsher all the time. When the coach stopped, we were plunged up to the heart in the night and the limpid silence; limpid . . . there's no other word for it. In that strange transparency the slightest sound attains its perfect timbre and its full sonority. We set out again into the night. Marceline was coughing. . . . Oh, wasn't she going to stop coughing? I thought back to the Sousse coach. It seemed to me that I was coughing better than that. She was making too much of an effort. How weak and changed she looked; in the dark, that way, I would hardly recognize her. How drawn her features were! Were the two dark openings of her nostrils always that conspicuous? Oh, it was terrible, the way she was coughing! That was the clearest result of her care for me. I loathe sympathy; it conceals every sort of contagion; one's sympathy should only be given to the strong. Oh, really, she was at the end of her rope! Wouldn't we get there soon? . . . What was she doing? . . . She took her handkerchief, raised it to her mouth, turned away. . . . My God, was she, too, going to cough up blood? Brutally, I tore the handkerchief out of her hands. In the pale light of the lantern, I looked at it. . . . Nothing. But I had showed my anxiety too openly; Marceline sadly tried to smile, murmuring: "No, not yet."

Finally we arrived. It was just in time; she could barely keep on going. The rooms that had been prepared for us didn't satisfy me; we would spend the night there, then change the next day. I found nothing good enough or too expensive. And, since the winter season hadn't begun, the vast hotel was nearly empty; I had my choice. I took two spacious, bright and simply furnished rooms; the large sitting room adjacent to them ended in a wide bow window with a view of both the hideous blue lake and some brutal mountain with sides that were either too heavily forested or too bare. That's where our meals were to be served. The suite was fantastically expensive, but what did I care! It's true, I no longer had my lecture course, but I was selling La Morinière. And after that we'd see. Anyway, what need had I for money? What need had I for all that? . . . I had now become strong. . . . I think that a complete change in one's fortunes should be just as educational as a complete change in one's health. . . . As for Marceline, she needed luxury; she was weak. . . . Oh, for her I would spend so much that — . . . And I was simultaneously acquiring both a taste and a distaste for that luxury. I washed and bathed my sensuality in it, then wished that that sensuality were a roving vagabond.

Meanwhile Marceline was feeling better, and my constant attentions were winning the day. Since she had difficulty eating, to stimulate her appetite I would order delicate, appealing dishes; we drank the best wines. I convinced myself that she was enjoying them greatly, because I myself was so delighted by those unfamiliar vintages we tried out daily. There were sharp Rhine wines, nearly syrupy tokays that filled me with their heady power. I remember a strange Barba Grisca, of which there was only one bottle left, so that I couldn't find out whether its funny taste would be repeated in the others.

Every day we rode out in a carriage, then, after snow had fallen, in a sleigh, wrapped in furs up to our neck. I would come back with a burning face and a keen appetite, leading to a good night's sleep. Meanwhile, I hadn't given up all my work, and found more than an hour daily in which to meditate on what I felt I had to say. It was no longer a question of history; for some time now my historical studies had no longer interested me except as a means for psychological research. I've told you how I had been able to renew my liking for the past when I thought I could see vague resemblances in it to my present state of mind; I had dared to hope that, by importuning the dead, I could obtain from them some secret tips about life. . . . Now, even young Athalaric could rise from his tomb to speak to me, and I would no longer listen to the past. Besides, how could an antiquated reply have satisfied my new question? "What is man still capable of?" That's what I needed to know. "Is what man has said up to now all he was able to say? Hasn't he been unaware of any part of himself? Is repeating old things all that's left for him?" . . . And every day there grew in me the confused presentiment of untouched riches that were covered up, hidden and stifled by civilizations, rules of propriety and moral codes.

It seemed to me at that time that I was born for an unknown kind of discovery; and with a strange ardor I pursued my shadowy researches, for which I know that the researcher had to abjure and cast away civilization, propriety and morals.

It was coming to the point when all I appreciated in others was a display of the most primitive values, regretting that any kind of constraint could repress them. I came near viewing decency as nothing but restrictions, conventions or fear. I would have liked to cherish it like some rare thing, difficult to achieve; our mode of life had turned it into the mutually binding, banal form of a contract. In Switzerland, it's an element of comfortable living. I understood Marceline's need of it, but I didn't conceal from her the new direction my ideas were taking. Already in Neuchâtel, when she was lauding that decency which emanates there from the walls of the buildings and the faces of the people, I countered: "My own is quite sufficient for me; I loathe decent people. If I have nothing to fear from them, I have nothing to learn from them, either. And, besides, *they* have nothing to tell me. . . . Decent Swiss folk! Their good health does them no good . . . without crimes, without a history, without a literature, without arts . . . a flourishing rosebush with neither thorns nor flowers. . . ."

And that this decent country would bore me, I knew beforehand, but after two months that boredom became a kind of fury, and all I could think about was leaving.

It was mid-January. Marceline was feeling better, much better; the continuous low fever that had been slowly sapping her strength was gone; there was a fresher glow to her cheeks; she enjoyed walking again, though not excessively; she was no longer as constantly weary as she had been. I didn't have too much trouble convincing her that she had derived all the benefit possible from that bracing air, and that now nothing could be better for her than to go down into Italy, where the mildness of the springtime would cure her completely — and I had no trouble convincing myself, above all, since I was so tired of those mountain heights.

And yet, now that, in my idleness, the hated past is garnering strength again, it's those memories especially that obsess me. Swift sleighrides; the merry nip of the dry air; getting spattered with snow; my hearty appetite; a groping walk in the mist, the strange tones of people's voices, the sudden emergence of objects; time spent reading in the snug sitting room; the landscape seen through the window, a frozen landscape; the tragic expectation of the snow; the disappearance of the outside world;

curling up voluptuously with my thoughts. . . . Oh, to go skating with her again, back there, alone, on that little clear lake lost in its encircling larches; then to return to the hotel with her in the evening. . . .

To me that descent into Italy was as dizzying as a fall. The weather was fine. As we sank into the milder and denser air, the rigid trees of the peaks, regularly spaced larches and firs, gave way to a rich vegetation of soft grace and ease. I felt as if I were leaving some realm of abstraction and reentering real life, and even though it was winter, I imagined fragrances everywhere. For much too long we had merely smiled at shadows. My deprivation was intoxicating me, and I was drunk with thirst as others are drunk with wine. The savings my life had stored away were remarkable; on the threshold of this tolerant and promising land, all my appetites burst forth. An enormous reserve of love filled me; at times it spread from my very depths to my head and made my thoughts shameless.

That illusion of springtime was transitory. The sudden change in altitude had managed to fool me for a moment, but once we had left the sheltered shores of the lakes, Bellagio, Como — where we lingered a few days — we found winter and rain again. The cold, which we had withstood well in the Engadine, was now no longer dry and light as in the mountains, but dank and depressing, and it started to make us ill. Marceline began coughing again. Then, to escape the cold, we moved farther south; we left Milan for Florence, Florence for Rome, Rome for Naples, which, in the winter rain, is surely the most cheerless city I know. My boredom was indescribable. We returned to Rome to look for a semblance of comfort, since we couldn't find warmth. On Monte Pincio we rented an apartment that was far too large, but admirably situated. Even when we were in Florence, we had been dissatisfied with the hotels and had taken a three-month lease on an exquisite villa on the Viale dei Colli. Other people might have wanted to live there forever. . . . We stayed there only three weeks. But at every new stage of our journey, I took care to set up house as if we would never leave. A stronger demon drove me on. . . . On top of that, we had with us no fewer than eight trunks. There was one filled with nothing but books and, during the entire trip, I didn't open it once.

I wouldn't allow Marceline to be involved in our expenses or try to reduce them. Of course I knew they were excessive, and that they couldn't go on that way. I stopped counting on money from La Morinière; the estate was no longer bringing in anything and Bocage wrote saying he couldn't find a purchaser. But all thoughts of the future only resulted in making me spend more. "Oh, why will I need so much, once I'm left alone?" I thought, and, full of anguish and expectation, I watched Marceline's frail life fading away even faster than my fortune.

Even though she left all worries to me, those frequently recurring moves from place to place were tiring her; but what wore her out the most, I now dare to admit it to myself, was her fear of my ideas.

One day she said to me: "I can see your doctrine and understand it — because it *is* a doctrine by now. It may be beautiful — " Then she added, more quietly, sadly, "but it does away with the weak."

"Which is what is wanted," I replied at once, despite myself.

Then I seemed to feel that delicate creature cringe and tremble at the horror of my brutal utterance. . . . Oh, maybe you'll conclude that I didn't love Marceline. I swear that I loved her ardently. She had never been so beautiful or seemed more beautiful to me. Her illness had re-fined and, as it were, exalted her features. I was now almost always by her side, lavishing constant attention on her, protecting her, guarding each instant of both her days and her nights. No matter how lightly she slept, I trained my sleep to remain even lighter; I watched her doze off and I awoke before she did. When, at times, I left her for an hour, wishing to walk by myself in the countryside or on the streets, some loving concern, or some fear that she might be bored, quickly called me back to her side; and sometimes I called upon my willpower, protesting against that hold over me, saying to myself: "Is that all you're good for, you would-be great man!" and I would force myself to prolong my absence; but then I would come back with my arms laden with flowers, early-blooming garden flowers or else hothouse flowers. . . . Yes, I tell you, I cherished her dearly. But how can I explain this? As I grew to respect myself less, I revered her more — and who can say how many passions and how many conflicting thoughts can coexist in a man? . . .

For some time now the bad weather had been over; springtime was arriving, and suddenly the almond trees broke into blossom. It was the first of March. In the morning I went down to the Piazza di Spagna. The peasants had stripped the countryside of its white boughs, and almond blossoms filled the vendors' baskets. I was so delighted that I bought a large bunch. Three men brought it to me. I returned to our apartment with all that springtime. The branches caught in the doorways, petals fell like snow on the carpet. I put some everywhere, into every vase; I turned the sitting room white with them, Marceline being out for the moment. Already I was rejoicing at her joy. . . . I heard her coming. There she was. She opened the door. She tottered. . . . She broke out sobbing.

"What's wrong? Poor Marceline!"

I busied myself with her, covered her with tender caresses. Then, as if to apologize for her tears, she said: "The fragrance of those flowers hurts me."

And it was a subtle, subtle, discreet honeylike fragrance. . . . Without a word, I seized those innocent, fragile branches, broke them, carried them out and threw them away, exasperated, my eyes bloodshot. Oh, if she could no longer abide even that little touch of springtime! . . .

I often think back to those tears and I now believe that, already knowing she was doomed, it was her regret for future springtimes that made her cry. I also think that there are strong joys for the strong, and weak joys for the weak, whom the strong joys would harm. As for her, she would grow tipsy at the slightest bit of pleasure; add a bit more dazzle, and she could no longer stand it. What she called happiness, I called repose, and, as for me, I wouldn't and couldn't rest.

Four days later we set out again for Sorrento. I was disappointed at not finding warmer weather there. Everything seemed to be shivering. The wind, which wouldn't stop blowing, wore Marceline out a good deal. We had decided to stop at the same hotel as on our last trip; we found the same room again. . . . With surprise, we discovered that the dreary sky had stolen the enchantment from the whole decor, making dismal the hotel garden that we had found so charming when we had walked in it as lovers.

We determined to go by sea to Palermo, whose climate was recommended to us; we returned to Naples, where we were to take the boat, and spent some more time there. But at Naples at least I wasn't bored. Naples is a living city where the past doesn't weigh heavily upon you.

Almost every moment of the day I stayed with Marceline. At night she went to bed early, since she was tired; I watched her fall asleep and sometimes went to bed myself; then, when I could tell from her more regular breathing that she was asleep, I would get up noiselessly, get dressed again in the dark, and sneak outside like a thief.

Outside! Oh, I could have shouted with gladness! What was I going to do? I didn't know. The sky, which had been dark during the day, was now cloudless; the moon, nearly full, was gleaming. I would walk randomly, without a goal, without a desire, without a constraint. I would look at everything with fresh eyes; I would listen for every sound with a more attentive ear; I would inhale the dampness of the night; I would place my hand on objects; I would prowl about.

The last evening we stayed in Naples, I prolonged that orgy of tramping until morning. When I was back I found Marceline in tears.

She had been afraid, she told me, having suddenly awakened and not having found me there. I calmed her down, did my best to explain my absence and promised not to leave her again. But on the very first night in Palermo, I couldn't control myself; I went out. . . . The first orange trees were blossoming; the slightest breeze carried their fragrance. . . .

We stayed in Palermo only five days; then, by a very round-about route, we returned to Taormina, which we both wanted to revisit. I think I told you that the village is perched quite high up in the hills; the railroad station is by the seashore. The carriage that brought us to the hotel had to take me right back to the station, where I was going to claim our trunks. I had stood up in the carriage to chat with the driver. He was a young Sicilian from Catania, handsome as a verse by Theocritus, bursting with health, fragrant, savory as a fruit.

"Com'è bella la signora!" he said, in a charming voice, as he watched Marceline walk away.

"Anche tu sei bello, ragazzo," I replied; and, since I was leaning toward him, I couldn't help myself and soon, drawing him toward me, I kissed him. He laughed and let me do so.

"I Francesi sono tutti amanti," he said.

"Ma non tutti gli Italiani amati," I countered, also laughing. . . . I looked for him on the days that followed, but never managed to see him again.*

We left Taormina for Syracuse. Step by step we were unraveling our first journey in reverse, returning toward the beginning of our love. And just as, during that first journey, I had made progress from week to week in reestablishing my health, so now from week to week, as we moved farther south, Marceline's condition was worsening.

What mental aberration, what stubborn blindness, what willful folly made me persuade myself and, above all, try to persuade her that she needed even more light and warmth, reminding her of my convalescence at Biskra? . . . And yet the air had become milder; the bay of Palermo enjoys clement weather and Marceline liked it there. There, she might have . . . But was I free to choose my own wishes, to decide upon my own desire?

At Syracuse the roughness of the sea and the irregularity of the boat service compelled us to wait a week. Every moment I didn't spend with Marceline, I spent in the old port. Oh, that little port in Syracuse!

---

* Translation of the four Italian sentences: "How beautiful the lady is!" . . . "You're beautiful too, my boy" . . . "All Frenchmen are lovers" . . . "But not all Italians are beloved."

The odors of soured wine, the muddy alleys, the stinking wineshop frequented by stevedores, tramps and drunken sailors! The company of the most degraded people delighted me. And what need had I of understanding their manner of speech, when all of my flesh enjoyed it? There, in my eyes, the brutality of passion still took on a hypocritical semblance of health and vigor. And it was no use telling myself that their wretched life couldn't be as enjoyable for them as it was for me. . . . Oh, I'd have liked to roll under the table with them and not awaken until the sad shudder of the morning. And in their company I intensified my growing hatred for luxury, comfort, for all I had surrounded myself with, the protection which my new-found health had rendered needless to me, all those precautions people take to preserve their body from dangerous contact with life. My imagination delved further into their existence. I'd have liked to pursue them further, to enter into their drunkenness. . . . Then suddenly I would recall Marceline. What was she doing at that moment? She was feeling ill, crying perhaps. . . . I would stand up hastily; I would run; I would return to the hotel, which seemed to have a sign over its door: "No poor people wanted here."

Marceline would always greet me the same way, without a word of blame or suspicion, and making an effort to smile in spite of everything. We took our meals by ourselves; I had them serve her all the best that the mediocre hotel could supply. And during the meal I would think: "A bit of bread and cheese, a fennel stalk is enough for them and would be just as sufficient for me. And maybe over there, quite close to us, there are some who are hungry and don't have even that meager pittance. . . . And here on my table is enough to glut them for three days!" I'd have liked to break down the walls and let the guests rush in. . . . And I would go back to the old port, where I would distribute at random the small coins with which my pockets were filled.

Man's poverty is slavish; in order to eat, it accepts unpleasurable work; any work that isn't happy is lamentable, I thought, and I subsidized the idleness of several people. I would say: "So don't work; it bores you." I desired each one of them to enjoy the leisure without which no novelty, no vice, no art can develop.

Marceline wasn't mistaken about my ideas; whenever I came back from the old port, I didn't conceal from her the fact that I had surrounded myself with quite shabby people. "A man contains the potential for everything." Marceline had a good glimpse of what I was ardently striving to discover; and when I reproached her for believing all too often in virtues that she herself discovered for the occasion in every living being, she said to me:

"You, you're only happy when you've made them display some vice. Don't you understand that our personal view of every man intensifies and exaggerates the traits in him that attract our attention? We make him become what we insist he is."

I would have been pleased to find her mistaken, but I still had to admit to myself that the worst instincts of everyone I met seemed to me the most sincere. Besides, what did I mean by sincerity?

We finally left Syracuse. The memory of, and desire for, the south obsessed me. At sea, Marceline felt better. . . . I recall the tone of the sea. It was so calm that the ship's wake seemed permanent. I still hear the sounds of dripping, the liquid sounds, the swabbing of the deck and the slapping of the swabbers' bare feet on the planks. I recall Malta, all white; the approach to Tunis. . . . How different I was!

It was hot, the weather was fine. Everything was splendid. Oh, I'd like an entire harvest of sensual pleasure to be distilled in every sentence here. . . . It would be useless to try now to impose upon my narrative more order than there was in my life. Long enough now I've tried to tell you how I became what I am. Oh, if I could only unburden my mind of this unbearable logic! . . . I feel nothing in myself but nobility.

Tunis. A light more copious than strong. Even the shade was filled with it. The air itself seemed like a luminous fluid in which everything was bathed, into which you dived, in which you swam. That voluptuous land satisfies your desire but doesn't quench it, and every new satisfaction merely heightens it.

A land lacking works of art. I have contempt for those who can't recognize beauty until it is transcribed and completely interpreted. The Arab people have the admirable trait of living their art, singing it and squandering it with no thought for the morrow; they don't petrify it or embalm it in any work of art. That is the reason for, and the result of, the absence of great artists. . . . I have always thought that those artists are truly great who dare to proclaim the beauty of things so natural that they make the viewer say afterward: "Why didn't I realize until then that that, too, was beautiful? . . ."

At Qairouan, with which I was still unfamiliar and where I went without Marceline, the night was very beautiful. At the moment of returning to my hotel to go to bed, I remembered a group of Arabs sleeping outdoors on mats outside a small café. I stretched out and slept right next to them. I came back covered with vermin.

Since the damp heat of the coast was weakening Marceline a great deal, I convinced her that the best thing for us was to reach Biskra as quickly as possible. It was the beginning of April.

That journey is a very long one. On the first day we got as far as Constantine in a single stage; on the second day, Marceline was very tired and we went only as far as El Kantara. There we sought and, toward evening, we found a shade more delectable and cool than moonlight at night. It was like an inexhaustible well; it trickled toward us. And from the slope where we were seated, we saw the plain ablaze. That night Marceline couldn't sleep; the strangeness of the silence and the slightest sounds troubled her. I was afraid she had some fever. I heard her tossing on her bed. The next day I thought she was paler. We departed.

Biskra. So that was where I wanted to get to. . . . Yes, there was the public park, the bench. . . . I recognized the bench on which I had sat during the first days of my convalescence. What was it I was reading there? . . . Homer; since then I haven't opened up that book again. There was the tree whose bark I went over to feel. How weak I was then! Ha! There were some children. . . . No, I didn't recognize any of them. How solemn Marceline was! She had changed as much as I. Why was she coughing when the weather was so fine? There was the hotel. There were our rooms, our terraces. What was Marceline thinking? She didn't say a word to me. As soon as she got to her room, she stretched out on the bed; she was weary and said she wanted to sleep a little. I went out.

I didn't recognize the children, but the children recognized me. Informed of my arrival, they all came running. Could it really be them? What a disappointment! What had happened? They'd grown older in a terrible way. In just a little over two years — it wasn't possible. . . . What fatigues, what vices, what indolence had already stamped so much ugliness on faces that had been so glowing with youth? What base labors had so quickly warped those beautiful bodies? It was like a bankruptcy. . . . I questioned them. Bashir was a dishwasher in a café; Ashur was barely earning a few sous breaking stones on roads; Hammatar had lost an eye. Who would have thought it? Sadek had settled down; he was helping an older brother sell bread in the market; he seemed to have become stupid. Ajib had become a butcher in his father's shop; he was getting fat; he was ugly; he was rich; he no longer wanted to speak to his lower-class companions. . . . How dull honorable careers make people! Was I, then, going to find again among them what I hated among us? Bubaker? He was married. He wasn't even fifteen. It was grotesque. And yet, not so; I saw him again that evening. He explained that his marriage was only a sham. I think he was a terrible libertine. But he was drinking, losing his figure. . . . And so that was all that was left? See what life does to you! My unbearable sadness made me realize that it was largely to see them again that I had come back here. Menalcas was right: memory is an unfortunate invention.

And Moktir? Oh, he was just out of prison. He was keeping out of sight. The others no longer consorted with him. I wanted to see him again. He was the best-looking of them all; was he going to disappoint me, too? . . . They located him. They brought him to me. No! *He* didn't let me down. Even in my memory he had never looked so splendid. His strength and beauty were perfect. . . . Recognizing me, he smiled.

"Well, what were you doing before you went to jail?"

"Nothing."

"Were you stealing?"

He protested.

"What are you doing now?"

He smiled.

"Oh, Moktir! If you have nothing to do, you'll accompany us to Touggourt." And I was suddenly seized with the desire to go to Touggourt.

Marceline wasn't well; I didn't know what was taking place within her. When I got back to the hotel that evening, she pressed herself against me without a word, her eyes closed. Her wide sleeve, pushed up, revealed a scrawny arm. I caressed her and rocked her back and forth for some time, as if she were a child I wanted to lull to sleep. Was it love or anxiety or fever that made her tremble so? . . . Oh, maybe there was still time. . . . Wouldn't I stop? I had sought and found the quality that constituted my worth: a sort of obstinate insistence on the worst in me. But how would I manage to tell Marceline that we were leaving for Touggourt the next day? . . .

Now she was sleeping in the next room. The moon, which had risen much earlier, was now flooding the terrace. It shed a light that was nearly frightening. It was impossible to hide from it. My room had white floor tiles, and the moonlight was especially in evidence there. Its beams entered through the wide-open window. I recognized its brightness in the room, and the shadow cast on it by the door. Two years ago it had come even further in . . . yes, precisely as far as it was now reaching — when I had arisen, giving up all attempts to sleep. I leaned my shoulder against the jamb of that door. I recognized the immobility of the palm trees. . . . What words had I read that evening? . . . Oh, yes, Christ's words to Peter: "Now thou girdest thyself, and walkest whither thou wilt." Where was I walking? Where did I want to go? . . . I haven't mentioned to you that, one day, on this latest journey, from Naples I had gone to Paestum by myself. . . . Oh, I wanted to sob amid those stones!

Antique beauty was made manifest, simple, perfect, smiling — abandoned. Art was taking its leave of me, I felt it. To make way for what else? It was no longer a smiling harmony, as in the past. . . . I no longer knew what shadowy god I was serving. "O new god!" I thought, "vouchsafe me to know ever new breeds of men, unforeseen types of beauty."

The next day, at dawn, the stagecoach carried us off. Moktir was with us. Moktir was happy as a king.

Chegga, Kaf Ed Dar, El Meghaïer . . . dreary stops on a road drearier still and endless. And yet I confess I imagined those oases to be more luxuriant. But there was nothing more than stone and sand; then several dwarfed bushes with bizarre blossoms; here and there some tentative palm trees watered by a hidden spring. . . . I now preferred the desert to the oasis . . . the desert, that land of mortal glory and intolerable splendor. Man's efforts seemed ugly and wretched there. Now any other kind of landscape bores me.

"You love the inhuman," Marceline said. But how she herself looked about her, and with what avidity!

On the second day, the weather changed somewhat for the worse; that is, the wind sprang up and the horizon became dull. Marceline was ill; the sand we were breathing burned and irritated her throat; the overabundant light tired her eyes; that hostile landscape battered her. But now it was too late to go back. In a few hours we would be in Touggourt.

It's this last part of our journey, even though it's so recent, that I remember least well. I find it impossible now to recall the landscapes we saw on the second day, or what I did at first in Touggourt. But what I still remember is how impatient and hurried I was.

It had been very cold in the morning. Toward evening, a blazing-hot simoom sprang up. Marceline, worn out by the trip, had gone to bed as soon as we got there. I hoped to find a somewhat more comfortable hotel; our room was a fright; the sand, sun and flies had tarnished, soiled and faded everything. Having had almost no food since daybreak, I had a meal served at once; but Marceline found everything bad and I couldn't persuade her to touch a thing. We had brought along supplies for making tea. I busied myself with that ludicrous task. For dinner we had to be satisfied with a few cookies and that tea, which the salty water of the region lent its awful taste.

In a last semblance of virtue, I stayed with her until evening. And all at once I myself felt as if my strength were gone. A taste of ashes! Weariness! The sadness of that superhuman effort! I hardly dared look at her; I knew all too well that my eyes, instead of looking into hers, were going to stare horribly at the black pits of her nostrils; the expression on her fevered face was ghastly. She didn't look at me, either. I felt her anguish as if I were touching it. She coughed a lot, then fell asleep. At moments a brusque shudder made her shake.

The night might be very bad and, before it was too late, I wanted to know to whom I could turn. I went out. In front of the hotel door, the main square of Touggourt, the streets, the very atmosphere, were so strange that I thought it was someone else, not me, looking at them. After a few moments, I returned. Marceline was sleeping peacefully. I had been wrong to get scared; in that weird country, you imagine dangers everywhere; it was absurd. And, sufficiently reassured, I went out again.

A strange nocturnal activity in the square, people going by in silence; a clandestine gliding past of white burnooses. At moments the wind tore off scraps of strange music and brought them from who knows where. Someone came up to me. . . . It was Moktir. He told me he had been waiting for me, that he had been sure I would come out again. He laughed. He was familiar with Touggourt, came there often and knew where he was taking me. I let him lead me away.

We walked in the night; we entered a Moorish café; that's where the music was coming from. Arab women were dancing there — if that monotonous gliding can be called a dance. One of them took me by the hand; I followed her; she was Moktir's mistress; he accompanied us. . . . The three of us entered a narrow, deep room in which a bed was the only item of furniture. . . . A very low bed, on which we sat. A white rabbit, locked up in the room, was shy at first, then grew tamer, came over and ate out of Moktir's hand. We were brought coffee. Then, while Moktir was playing with the rabbit, that woman drew me toward her, and I yielded myself to her just as one drifts away into sleep. . . .

Ah! Here I could tell a false story or keep silent, but what good is this narrative to me if it ceases to be truthful? . . .

I returned to the hotel alone, Moktir staying in the café for the night. It was late. A dry scirocco was blowing: a wind laden with sand, and torrid even at night. After just a few steps I was soaking wet; but suddenly I was in an excessive hurry to reach the hotel, and I returned almost at a run. Maybe she had awakened. . . . Maybe she needed me. . . . No, the casement of the room was dark. Before opening the door I waited for a slight pause in the wind; I entered very softly into the blackness. What was that noise? . . . I didn't recognize her cough. . . . I turned on the light.

Marceline was on the bed, partially sitting up; one of her thin arms tightly clutched the bars of the bed, keeping her erect; her sheets, her hands, her nightgown were soaked in blood she had coughed up; her face was all smeared with it, her eyes were bulging horribly; and the shrillest cry of agony would have been less frightening to me than her silence. I scanned her perspiring face for a small spot on which to place a fearful kiss; the taste of her sweat remained on my lips. I washed and cooled her forehead and cheeks. . . . Beside the bed there was something hard under my foot: I stooped down and picked up the little rosary she had once asked for in Paris, and which she had now dropped; I placed it in her open hand, but her hand immediately sank and dropped it again. I didn't know what to do: I wanted to ask for help. . . . Her hand grasped me in desperation, holding me back. Oh! Did she think I wanted to leave her?

She said to me: "It won't hurt you to wait a little longer." Seeing that I wanted to speak, she added: "Don't say anything to me; all is well." Again I picked up the rosary; I put it back in her hand, but again she let it — no, she *made* it fall. I knelt down beside her and pressed her hand against me.

She let herself subside, partly onto the bolster, partly onto my shoulder; she seemed to sleep for a while, but her eyes remained wide open.

An hour later she raised herself again; her hand disengaged itself from my hands, tightened around her nightgown and ripped the lace there. She was suffocating. Toward the early morning, she spat up blood again. . . .

I have finished telling you my story. What more could I add? The French cemetary at Touggourt is hideous, half swallowed up in sand. . . . I used all the little willpower I had left to me to rescue her from that distressing spot. Her resting place is at El Kantara, in the shade of a private garden that she loved. Scarcely three months have gone by since those events. Those three months have made it seem like ten years ago.

Michel remained silent for some time. We kept still also, each of us prey to a strange uneasiness. It seemed to us, unfortunately, that by recounting his actions to us, Michel had made them more legitimate. Since, in the long explanation he gave for them, we didn't know at what point to express disapproval, we felt almost like accomplices. It was as if we were directly involved. He had finished that narrative without a quaver in his voice, without an inflection or gesture to indicate that any emotion whatsoever was troubling him — either because he took a cynical pride in not displaying emotion to us; or because, out of some feeling of reserve, he feared to arouse emotion in us by weeping; or else simply because he felt no emo-

tion. Even now I can't decide how much pride, strength, coldness or reserve entered into his feelings. After a moment he resumed:

What frightens me, I confess, is that I'm still very young. I sometimes feel as if my real life hasn't begun yet. Rescue me from this place now and give me reasons for living. *I* can no longer find any. I've won freedom, possibly, but what for? I'm suffering from this freedom that has no purpose. Believe me, it's not because I'm worn out by my crime, if you wish to call it that — but I must prove to myself that I didn't claim more than what was due to me.

When you first met me, my ideas were solidly established, and I know that that is what constitutes a real man; they no longer are. But I think this climate is the cause. Nothing discourages thought as much as these unchanging blue skies. Here no mental quest is possible, because sensual fulfillment follows so closely upon desire. Surrounded by splendor and death, I feel that happiness is too omnipresent, and self-abandonment to happiness is too readily available. I go to bed at noon to beguile the dreary length of the days and their unbearable lack of occupation.

Look, here I have some white pebbles which I soak in the shade and then hold in the hollow of my hand for a long time, until the calm I obtain from their coolness has worn off. Then I start all over again, alternating the pebbles, putting back into the shade those that are no longer cool. Time passes that way, and the evening comes. . . . Rescue me from this place; I can't do it on my own. Something in my willpower has snapped; I don't even know where I found the strength to leave El Kantara. Sometimes I'm afraid that the part of me I have suppressed is taking its revenge. I'd like to start afresh. I'd like to get rid of whatever fortune is left to me; look, these walls are still covered with it. . . . Here I live on next to nothing. An innkeeper who's partly French prepares a little food for me. The child who ran away as you came in brings it to me in the evening and in the morning, in exchange for a few sous and caresses. That child, who acts like a savage in front of strangers, is as loving and faithful to me as a dog. His sister is an Ouled-Naïl* who goes to Constantine every winter to sell her body to passers-by. She's very beautiful and, in the first weeks, I allowed her to spend occasional nights with me. But one morning her brother, little Ali, caught us in bed together. He was extremely vexed and refused to come back for five days.

---

* The girls of this tribal group traditionally earned their dowry through premarital prostitution.

And yet he knows very well how, and on what, his sister lives; earlier he had spoken of it in a tone that showed no embarrassment. . . . Was he jealous, then? Anyway, that scamp got what he wanted; because, partly from boredom and partly from fear of losing Ali, since that adventure I haven't kept that girl with me. She didn't get angry over it; but every time I meet her, she laughs and jokes about my preferring the boy to her. She claims that he's the main thing keeping me here. Maybe she's not altogether wrong. . . .

DOVER·THRIFT·EDITIONS

All books complete and unabridged. All 5³⁄₁₆″ × 8¼″, paperbound.
Just $1.00–$2.00 in U.S.A.

POETRY

GREAT LOVE POEMS, Shane Weller (ed.). 128pp. 27284-2 $1.00

SELECTED POEMS, Walt Whitman. 128pp. 26878-0 $1.00

THE BALLAD OF READING GAOL AND OTHER POEMS, Oscar Wilde. 64pp. 27072-6 $1.00

FAVORITE POEMS, William Wordsworth. 80pp. 27073-4 $1.00

EARLY POEMS, William Butler Yeats. 128pp. 27808-5 $1.00

FICTION

FLATLAND: A ROMANCE OF MANY DIMENSIONS, Edwin A. Abbott. 96pp. 27263-X $1.00

BEOWULF, Beowulf (trans. by R. K. Gordon). 64pp. 27264-8 $1.00

CIVIL WAR STORIES, Ambrose Bierce. 128pp. 28038-1 $1.00

ALICE'S ADVENTURES IN WONDERLAND, Lewis Carroll. 96pp. 27543-4 $1.00

O PIONEERS!, Willa Cather. 128pp. 27785-2 $1.00

FIVE GREAT SHORT STORIES, Anton Chekhov. 96pp. 26463-7 $1.00

FAVORITE FATHER BROWN STORIES, G. K. Chesterton. 96pp. 27545-0 $1.00

THE AWAKENING, Kate Chopin. 128pp. 27786-0 $1.00

HEART OF DARKNESS, Joseph Conrad. 80pp. 26464-5 $1.00

THE SECRET SHARER AND OTHER STORIES, Joseph Conrad. 128pp. 27546-9 $1.00

THE OPEN BOAT AND OTHER STORIES, Stephen Crane. 128pp. 27547-7 $1.00

THE RED BADGE OF COURAGE, Stephen Crane. 112pp. 26465-3 $1.00

A CHRISTMAS CAROL, Charles Dickens. 80pp. 26865-9 $1.00

THE CRICKET ON THE HEARTH AND OTHER CHRISTMAS STORIES, Charles Dickens. 128pp. 28039-X $1.00

NOTES FROM THE UNDERGROUND, Fyodor Dostoyevsky. 96pp. 27053-X $1.00

SIX GREAT SHERLOCK HOLMES STORIES, Sir Arthur Conan Doyle. 112pp. 27055-6 $1.00

WHERE ANGELS FEAR TO TREAD, E. M. Forster. 128pp. (Available in U.S. only) 27791-7 $1.00

THE OVERCOAT AND OTHER SHORT STORIES, Nikolai Gogol. 112pp. 27057-2 $1.00

GREAT GHOST STORIES, John Grafton (ed.). 112pp. 27270-2 $1.00

THE LUCK OF ROARING CAMP AND OTHER SHORT STORIES, Bret Harte. 96pp. 27271-0 $1.00

THE SCARLET LETTER, Nathaniel Hawthorne. 192pp. 28048-9 $2.00

YOUNG GOODMAN BROWN AND OTHER SHORT STORIES, Nathaniel Hawthorne. 128pp. 27060-2 $1.00

THE GIFT OF THE MAGI AND OTHER SHORT STORIES, O. Henry. 96pp. 27061-0 $1.00

THE NUTCRACKER AND THE GOLDEN POT, E. T. A. Hoffmann. 128pp. 27806-9 $1.00

THE BEAST IN THE JUNGLE AND OTHER STORIES, Henry James. 128pp. 27552-3 $1.00

THE TURN OF THE SCREW, Henry James. 96pp. 26684-2 $1.00

DUBLINERS, James Joyce. 160pp. 26870-5 $1.00

A PORTRAIT OF THE ARTIST AS A YOUNG MAN, James Joyce. 192pp. 28050-0 $2.00

DOVER · THRIFT · EDITIONS

All books complete and unabridged. All 5³⁄₁₆″ × 8¼″, paperbound.
Just $1.00–$2.00 in U.S.A.

FICTION

THE MAN WHO WOULD BE KING AND OTHER STORIES, Rudyard Kipling. 128pp. 28051-9 $1.00

SELECTED SHORT STORIES, D. H. Lawrence. 128pp. 27794-1 $1.00

GREEN TEA AND OTHER GHOST STORIES, J. Sheridan LeFanu. 96pp. 27795-X $1.00

THE CALL OF THE WILD, Jack London. 64pp. 26472-6 $1.00

FIVE GREAT SHORT STORIES, Jack London. 96pp. 27063-7 $1.00

WHITE FANG, Jack London. 160pp. 26968-X $1.00

THE NECKLACE AND OTHER SHORT STORIES, Guy de Maupassant. 128pp. 27064-5 $1.00

BARTLEBY AND BENITO CERENO, Herman Melville. 112pp. 26473-4 $1.00

THE GOLD-BUG AND OTHER TALES, Edgar Allan Poe. 128pp. 26875-6 $1.00

THE QUEEN OF SPADES AND OTHER STORIES, Alexander Pushkin. 128pp. 28054-3 $1.00

THREE LIVES, Gertrude Stein. 176pp. 28059-4 $2.00

THE STRANGE CASE OF DR. JEKYLL AND MR. HYDE, Robert Louis Stevenson. 64pp. 26688-5 $1.00

TREASURE ISLAND, Robert Louis Stevenson. 160pp. 27559-0 $1.00

THE KREUTZER SONATA AND OTHER SHORT STORIES, Leo Tolstoy. 144pp. 27805-0 $1.00

ADVENTURES OF HUCKLEBERRY FINN, Mark Twain. 224pp. 28061-6 $2.00

THE MYSTERIOUS STRANGER AND OTHER STORIES, Mark Twain. 128pp. 27069-6 $1.00

CANDIDE, Voltaire (François-Marie Arouet). 112pp. 26689-3 $1.00

THE INVISIBLE MAN, H. G. Wells. 112pp. (Available in U.S. only.) 27071-8 $1.00

ETHAN FROME, Edith Wharton. 96pp. 26690-7 $1.00

THE PICTURE OF DORIAN GRAY, Oscar Wilde. 192pp. 27807-7 $1.00

NONFICTION

THE DEVIL'S DICTIONARY, Ambrose Bierce. 144pp. 27542-6 $1.00

THE SOULS OF BLACK FOLK, W. E. B. Du Bois. 176pp. 28041-1 $2.00

SELF-RELIANCE AND OTHER ESSAYS, Ralph Waldo Emerson. 128pp. 27790-9 $1.00

GREAT SPEECHES, Abraham Lincoln. 112pp. 26872-1 $1.00

THE PRINCE, Niccolò Machiavelli. 80pp. 27274-5 $1.00

SYMPOSIUM AND PHAEDRUS, Plato. 96pp. 27798-4 $1.00

THE TRIAL AND DEATH OF SOCRATES: FOUR DIALOGUES, Plato. 128pp. 27066-1 $1.00

CIVIL DISOBEDIENCE AND OTHER ESSAYS, Henry David Thoreau. 96pp. 27563-9 $1.00

THE THEORY OF THE LEISURE CLASS, Thorstein Veblen. 256pp. 28062-4 $2.00

PLAYS

THE CHERRY ORCHARD, Anton Chekhov. 64pp. 26682-6 $1.00

THE THREE SISTERS, Anton Chekhov. 64pp. 27544-2 $1.00

THE WAY OF THE WORLD, William Congreve. 80pp. 27787-9 $1.00

MEDEA, Euripides. 64pp. 27548-5 $1.00

THE MIKADO, William Schwenck Gilbert. 64pp. 27268-0 $1.00